JUN 7 1991
PUBLIC LIBRARY

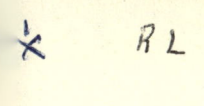

WITHDRAWN

LARGE PRINT   083717

ST. JAMES-ASSINIBOIA

GUNSMOKE IN NEVADA

Burt Arthur

The Nevada town of Paradise was wide open, ruled by the worst gang of cut-throats since Quantrill's raiders ripped up the West. Ex-Ranger Johnny Canavan was two hundred pounds of fighting man – one hundred pounds to each fist. He'd come to Paradise to clean up the town but there were fifty guns that said he wouldn't ride out any way but feet first!

OTHER LARGE PRINT BOOKS BY BURT ARTHUR

Boss of the Far West
Bugles in the Night
The Freelands

GUNSMOKE IN NEVADA

Burt Arthur

Curley Publishing, Inc.
South Yarmouth, Ma.

> **Library of Congress Cataloging-in-Publication Data**
>
> Arthur, Burt. 1899–1975.
>   Gunsmoke in Nevada / Burt Arthur.
>   p. cm.
>   "Curley large print."—T.p. verso.
>   1. Nevada—Paradise Valley—Fiction.   2. Large type books.
> I. Title.
>   [PS3501.R77G87   1990]
>   813'.52—dc20
>   ISBN 0-7927-0478-9 (lg. print)   90-30594
>   ISBN 0-7927-0479-7 (pbk.: lg. print)   CIP

Copyright © 1956 by Burt Arthur
Copyright renewed © 1984 Burt Arthur

All rights reserved. No part of this book may be used or reproduced in any manner without written permission except in the case of brief quotations embodied in critical articles and reviews.

Published in Large Print by arrangement with Donald MacCampbell, Inc. in the United States, Canada, the U.K. and British Commonwealth.

Distributed in Great Britain, Ireland and the Commonwealth by CHIVERS LIBRARY SERVICES LIMITED, Bath BA1 3HB, England.

Printed in Great Britain

GUNSMOKE IN NEVADA

I

It was late afternoon when Johnny Canavan, drumming steadily westward over the Nevada rangeland, topped some high ground and pulled up. He dismounted rather stiffly, grimacing a little too, and stamped about in an effort to ease the ache in the small of his back and the cramped feeling in his legs. It was a breather that Aggie, his mare, welcomed, for it marked their first halt since the middle of the morning. Evidence that the long, uninterrupted pull had exacted its toll of her was the way she stood blowing herself, spread-legged, her head bowed and sides heaving. Hand-shading his eyes, Canavan lifted his gaze in a hopeful, searching look of the open country. It spread away before him like a slightly scuffed-up and humpbacked greenish carpet with thin brownish tinges here and there in its far-flung expanse. There were tiny clusters of wild flowers dotting the range too, and their rich, sweet fragrance climbed above the stronger smell of the lush grass. He spotted the town off in the distance after a minute's scanning. It lay just below the level of the prairie in a sort of hand-scooped-out saucer of a valley that was the shallowest he had ever seen. When he wheeled around to the mare, startling her with the suddenness with which he moved, she sensed something of importance. She hoped it meant that he had found a town. In happy anticipation of what a town meant to her – food and water and a comfortable stall – she stood erect again. Eager to get to them, the moment she felt Canavan swing up astride her, she loped away with him. After a bit, she lengthened her stride and broke into a swift run, apparently forgetting her earlier weariness.

They came up to the signpost at the entrance to the town in a flurry of hoofbeats and a boiling-up of dust. Slacking in the saddle, Canavan eyed the sign critically. It was a picture of abandonment, slumping dejectedly in its over-sized hole in the ground. The rocks and stones that had once helped fill the hole and hold the post upright were strewn about. A single rusted nail held the crosspiece in place on the post, but it did not prevent the sign itself from slipping and pointing earthward instead of westward, the direction in which the town lay. Canavan bent sideways, craning his neck in an effort to make out the legend on the crosspiece. But after a minute's futile study of it, he gave up. The letters were so badly sunfaded, they were no longer readable. Straightening up, he nudged Aggie with his knees, and the mare, pawing the ground impatiently, trotted on. A span of trampled, churned-up ground, and then a downgrade, led to the town.

Taking the downgrade, Aggie's iron-shod hoofs produced a carrying metallic clatter as she pranced over the shale-and-stone surfacing. Like most cattle towns, this one too, Canavan noted in a swift ranging glance, consisted of a single street. The wheel-rutted gutter, the narrow, planked walks and low wooden curbs; the hitch rails and step-down blocks, the shoulder-to-shoulder rows of shacks, houses and stores, all weather-beaten and drab-looking, and all so badly in need of painting, all were typical of the average cattle town. In the main the street itself ran fairly straight. It was only when it stretched away toward the far corner that it seemed to veer off unexplainably and curve a little. The offending span, Canavan decided, was doubtless newer than the original street. It had probably been added in haste with the arrival of more and more people and the need for more dwellings and more commercial establishments to serve them.

Canavan was surprised, then dismayed, to find the street deserted. His first thought was that he had come upon a ghost town.

It came as a bitter disappointment to him, for here, once he had found the place, he had hoped to be able to replenish his nearly exhausted supply of coffee, bacon and flour. Unconsciously he felt behind him for his saddlebags. They were almost flat to the touch. When he drew his hand away, they slapped emptily against the mare's sides. But in that same moment of disappointment he realized that the usual signs of abandonment were missing. Instead he spotted evidences of repairs, proof that it wasn't a ghost town, and his eager, probing eyes took quick note of them. They were little things that someone else, someone who was not as observant, might not have noticed, such as a new doorstep, some nail heads that gleamed with unmistakable newness, and a fairly recently washed windowpane that had been weather-proofed by edging the inner part of the frame with freshly melted wax.

Despite the fact that the shop doors on both sides of the strangely hushed street were closed, he caught fleeting glimpses here and there of faces peering out at him rather stealthily, he thought, from above the tops of the store windows' half-curtains. There was something wrong, he told himself, and he wondered what it was. Then, when they were about midway up the street, Aggie suddenly stopped. Instinctively Canavan raised his eyes and just as promptly caught his breath.

Hanging at the looped and knotted end of a short cut of rope, which in turn hung from a wooden arm that jutted out over the planked walk from the flat roof of a one-story building, was the dangling figure of a wrist- and ankle-bound man. The mare whinnied and nervously pawed the ground, and backed a little, as though she recognized the nearness of death and had no desire to get any closer to it than she had to. Canavan leaned down and patted her and spoke to her, and after a bit she plodded on again. When they came abreast of the hanged man, Canavan reined in, slacked back in the saddle and looked up. Death was no stranger to him. He had seen much of it. The tied-down gun that rode low on his lean right thigh had dealt out a fair share of it. But there was something pathetic about the dangling figure. His boots were badly scuffed and worn through. His levis were faded, threadbare in some spots and patched in others. His shirt was in keeping with the rest of his shabbiness, washed-out-looking and too small for him. He looked like a man who had wallowed in adversity only to meet his end in about as miserable a way as it was possible to imagine. Without knowing the man or why he had been hanged, Canavan couldn't help but feel sorry for him. But death was final, sympathy notwithstanding, and what was done was done. With a grim shake of his head, Canavan rode on. He looked back once, when he heard the wooden arm and the rope creak. There was no breeze, no apparent reason for it, yet he saw the dangling body twist around gently in a half-circle. But then it stopped, and it hung motionlessly again.

Nearing the far corner, Canavan spied a sign over a doorway that read HOTEL, and he guided Aggie over to the low curb, followed it and stopped her when they came up to the place. He swung down, lifted his saddlebags off the mare's back and hoisted them to his shoulder, stepped up on the walk, crossed it and went into the hotel. A thin-faced man with a shiny bald head was behind the counter that served as a desk. He looked up when he heard Canavan's step, held his gaze on Canavan as the latter strode up to the counter.

"What'll it be, Mister?" he asked. "Room or bath?"

"Both," Canavan replied.

"That'll be a dollar and a half."

Canavan slapped a couple of silver pieces on the counter. The man picked them up, put them in his pants pocket.

"Room Two, top o' the stairs. Tub's out in

the barn. So's the bucket. Soon's you're ready for it, lemme know and I'll show you where to get the water."

Canavan nodded.

"What's the name of this town?" he asked.

"Paradise," he was told.

"Paradise?" Canavan echoed. "Never expected to see a hanging in Paradise. Thought everything was supposed to be nice and friendly and peaceful there. Must be this isn't the Paradise I was thinking of, huh?"

There was no comment, only a flat statement.

"There's another hanging set for tomorrow morning."

"You don't say!"

"We've been averaging about one a month for the past seven months or so."

"What's the idea? Too much population, and hanging folks the best way to hold it down to size?"

The man smiled thinly. But as before, he made no comment, and Canavan turned and took the stairs to the upper floor.

It was evening, just about eight-thirty, and the long-fingered shadows were beginning to give way to darkness. Canavan was standing at the raised window in his hotel room, staring down moodily into the street. Minutes before he had poked his head out, wondering if the hanged man was still dangling at the end of the noose; apparently he had been cut down for the noose hung limply open. A foot or two behind Canavan, and backed against the side wall, was a bureau, and atop the bureau was a lighted lamp. A sudden gust of wind came swirling into the room and made the light flicker. Canavan turned his head and glanced at it. But just as suddenly as it had come, the wind seemed to have gone, dissolved into nothingness, for the light steadied and burned evenly. Then just as he was about to square around again to the window, he heard heavy, scuffing footsteps on the stairs, heard them too a moment later on the bare, warped landing floor. Then they came up to his door and stopped, and he heard a low murmuring outside it. He saw the knob turn, saw the door open, watched it open even wider, and he frowned. Then it was pushed back, and a big, burly man with a heavy-featured and unshaven face was looking in at him over the threshold. Canavan glimpsed two other men behind the first one.

"Mind if we come in, Mac?"

Canavan's eyes were hard, his mouth tightened.

"Yeah, I mind."

The full, almost thick lips in the stubbled

face parted in a grin, and the big man said over his shoulder in a rather mocking tone:

"He minds."

"Well, now, ain't that too damned bad?" a man behind him said with a short, scornful laugh. "Go 'head, Mike. Go on in."

The man named Mike sauntered inside. He was so thick-legged he lumbered rather than walked. He made Canavan think of a bear he had once seen. Mike's companions trooped in at his heels. The first one of the two, the man who had laughed, a dark, thin-faced man with quick, darting eyes framed in it, closed the door and backed against it; the other man, a solidly built, lighter-complexioned and round-faced individual, drifted past it and stopped, and both stood a little spread-legged with their thumbs hooked in their gunbelts. Mike halted when he came abreast of the bureau. He glanced at the lamp, reached up and turned the wick, lowering the light, looked around the room, nodded and said:

"That's better." Then facing Canavan: "What brings you to Paradise, Mac?"

"Just passing through," was Canavan's simple reply.

"Oh! Where you headed?"

"California."

"And where you from?"

"O-o-oh, different places."

"What d'you do?"

"Whatever strikes my fancy."

The dark-faced man scowled. He straightened up and said curtly: "Don't get smart, Mister."

Mike thumbed his hat up from his forehead. The sweatband was tight and left a thin, red, almost angry-looking line across his forehead and temples. When he rubbed his forehead with the back of his hand, the line was erased but the redness spread.

"What's your name?"

"Smith, I'll bet," the man at the door said.

"How'd you guess?" Canavan asked.

The man glowered a little and said: "You're just a mite too slick with your tongue, Mister. You keep answering in that smart-alecky way and you'll be sorry."

"Take it easy, Vasco," Mike said over his thick shoulder. "You hightailing it, Mac?"

"You the law?" Canavan countered.

"Nope."

"Then wouldn't you say that's a kind of personal matter and none of your business?"

"Oh, is he askin' for a good walloping!" Vasco said.

"Yeah," the man next to him added. "Just begging for it."

"Mister," Vasco said. "We don't like your

kind around Paradise. Get your gear and get outta here."

Canavan paid no attention to him.

"You heard me, didn't you?" Vasco demanded, and his dark face was suddenly red-splotched.

"Keep your shirt on, Vasco," Mike told him, half-turning to him.

"It's all right," Canavan said. "Let him spout. He doesn't scare me any."

Apparently Vasco went for his gun for Mike suddenly leaped at him, pinned him against the door and held him there.

"Told you to take it easy, didn't I? Now watch it, y'hear?" Mike released Vasco and turned again to Canavan. "How long you aiming to stay around, Mac?"

"Don't know yet."

"If you're looking to get in on a nice set-up, we've got a spot for you, Mac."

"Thanks, but I don't think I'm interested."

"No harm in you thinking about it though. And if you want to know more about it, what we've got to offer, you can find me down at the saloon. Name's Hoban. Mike Hoban."

Canavan didn't answer; apparently he wasn't expected to for Mike turned again and walked doorward. Vasco stepped aside and Mike opened the door and went out. He turned in the landing.

"All right, you fellers. Come on. Vasco, Russ."

The man whom Mike had called Russ looked questioningly at Vasco; when the latter jerked his head in the direction of the door, Russ nodded and trudged out. Canavan saw him walk off after Mike.

"What do you say, Vasco?" Mike called from a short distance away, probably from the head of the stairs, Canavan judged.

"You fellers go ahead, Mike," Vasco answered. "I'll catch up with you."

Mike came striding back to the open doorway.

"What's the idea?" he wanted to know.

"You mind if I kinda visit for a minute or so with our friend here?"

Mike frowned.

"I told you to watch it, Vasco," he said evenly. "You step outta line and —"

"Like I've heard the judge tell you a couple o' times, Mike," the dark-faced man interrupted, "don't always go getting ahead of yourself."

Mike wheeled away and went striding down the landing. A moment later Canavan heard him, then a somewhat lighter-stepping man go down the stairs. Vasco closed the door and backed against it. He reached down and drew a long, thin-bladed knife out of his boot, slapped the blade against the palm of his left hand a couple of times and looked up.

"I can hit a running man from thirty feet away with this," he said and he smiled a little thinly. "That oughta give you a pretty good idea of what I can do with it from only ten feet away."

There was no response from the motionless Canavan.

"Now if you don't want me to prove to you how good I am with this," Vasco went on, holding up the knife and gesturing with it, "see to it that you're gone before I'm up and around tomorrow morning. If I hear you're still around, I'll come looking for you. Now I don't have to tell you what'll happen to you then, do I?"

He had stopped gesturing for the moment and was holding the knife upright in mid-air. Canavan's right arm moved so suddenly, so swiftly too, that his draw, so perfectly executed, was just a blurry motion of lightning-like handwork to Vasco. Canavan's gun seemed to leap into his hand. It roared deafeningly. Vasco jerked backward instinctively and bumped the door. Then he stared hard at his right hand. He was still holding the knife handle. But the blade was gone, sheared off cleanly. He looked down. The blade lay at his feet, squarely between them. There were heavy, running bootsteps on the stairs. Vasco, still dazed and still gripped by the magic of Canavan's lightning draw and expert shooting, was sent careening away when the door was flung open. Framed in the doorway was panting, chest-heaving Mike Hoban. The man crowding up behind him and peering over Mike's shoulder was Russ.

"What ... what's going on here?" Hoban demanded, still struggling to get his breath.

"Nothing much," Canavan answered, holstering his gun. "We were just showing off to each other, me with my gun and your side-kick over there with his knife."

"H'm," Mike said, but there was disbelief in his voice. He crossed the threshold, stopped instantly when he stepped on the broken-off knife blade and stepped back again and looked down. He leveled a hard look at Vasco, lashed out with his foot and kicked the blade, sent it spinning across the room. It disappeared under the bed. "All right, Vasco. Let's go."

Vasco hitched up his pants, looked at Canavan over his shoulder and said: "I'll be looking for you, Mister. We've got a little something to settle."

"I'll be around," Canavan responded.

Vasco tossed the knife handle on the bed and stalked out; Hoban and then Russ moved aside to let him pass. When Mike gestured,

Russ turned and walked off after Vasco. Then Hoban too, without a word to Canavan, strode out. Canavan crossed to the door and closed it. From his window he watched the three men go downstreet; when he couldn't see them any longer, he turned away from the window and seated himself on the edge of the bed. But a minute later he was on his feet again. He blew out the light in the lamp and strode out of the room, curling his hat brim with his hands as he walked down the stairs. Emerging from the hotel, he stood in front of it briefly, glanced diagonally across the street in the direction of the stable where he had left Aggie, then with a lift of his shoulders, sauntered downstreet. As he came abreast of a store with a boarded-up front he glanced at it curiously, slowing his step unconsciously. A voice called to him and he stopped, backed a couple of steps till he came to the doorway. A stocky man with turned-down lamplight burning somewhere behind him stood in the doorway.

"Yeah?" Canavan asked. "You call me?"

"Yes. My name is Daws. Christopher Daws. It mean anything to you?"

"Daws?" Canavan repeated. "No-o, 'fraid not, partner. Is it supposed to?"

"Sorry. I mistook you for someone else."

Canavan stepped closer to the doorway. It

enabled him to see inside the store. The dimmed lamplight left the place shadowy, even dark in the corners. He saw a press backed against a long, blank, whitewashed wall, and he glimpsed other pieces of printing equipment and a roll-top desk. Square sheets of cut paper were stacked up on a small wooden platform a step beyond the desk.

"What d'you do here?" he asked. "Put out a newspaper?"

"That's right. The *Paradise Clarion*."

"Uh-huh. What is it, a weekly thing?"

"Yes, when we publish."

"Y'mean there's no set time for putting it out?"

"We used to publish on Thursdays."

"And now?"

"The paper hasn't gone to press in some seven months now," was the simple reply.

Canavan looked obliquely at the man.

"S'matter?" he asked. "Haven't you got enough readers to make putting it out worthwhile?"

"Oh, we have the readers, all right."

"Then how come . . . ?"

"When a newspaper isn't free to speak its mind, there isn't any point in publishing it."

"No-o, I suppose not," Canavan conceded. Then he suggested: "Sounds to me like somebody didn't like what you were saying in your paper."

"He didn't like it at all," was the blunt response.

"Smashing in your window his way of telling you that?"

"Yes," Daws acknowledged. His eyes ranged over Canavan. "Sa-ay, you're a pretty big fellow."

"Got a couple of brothers who are even bigger."

"They must be giants."

"We-ll, not exactly giants," Canavan answered gravely. "Just good-sized. Just over six-four. I'm a shade the other way. Under it."

The stocky man smiled, a little sadly, Canavan thought.

"I saw you come into town this afternoon," the newspaper publisher related. "Planning to stay on in Paradise?"

"No. I'm on my way to California."

"Oh," Daws said, and there was no mistaking the disappointment in his tone. "I had hoped you might decide to stay on here. You haven't that hunted furtive look about you that Harp's followers have, and that in itself would make you a welcome addition to our population. However, since you have other plans . . ."

"Who was that you said? Harp?"

"Yes, Judge Harp. Judge Lucius Harp."

"Who's he?"

"He runs Paradise."

"Oh! Was it on account of him that you had to close up shop?"

Daws nodded.

"Think you said you haven't put out your paper in some seven months now. That when this Harp took over the town?"

"That's right. And things haven't been the same here since. He came into Paradise one day with a handful of questionable-looking, hard-eyed characters, announced he'd been sent here by the governor, and opened an office for himself. On his office wall he hung a framed certificate of appointment, so there wasn't any question as to his authority. The next thing we knew, Tom Kane who owned the saloon was gone and the judge was there instead."

"He buy this Kane out, or kick him out?"

"No one seems to know exactly what happened. Anyway, Harp gave up his rented office and made the back room of the saloon his headquarters. It soon became the center of all activity here," Daws related, and there was bitterness, contempt too, in his thickening voice, "with everyone beating a path to the judge's door. No one could do anything on his own. Everyone, it seemed, had to consult the judge first. It was a little ridiculous. However, people, by and large, are pretty much like sheep. They see one person do something and they too have to do it. Anyway, shortly after Harp took over the town, some homesteaders came into Paradise. The name must have fooled them, made them think they'd finally found a haven, a refuge for themselves. But you probably know how unwelcome homesteaders are in cattle country."

"Yeah," Canavan said grimly. "I know."

"Almost immediately there was friction between them and the cattlemen. At first there were just muttered grumblings on the part of the ranchers. Then there were threats of violence if the homesteaders didn't clear out. When they refused to be cowed, the threats erupted into violence of the worst kind, daily beatings, shootings and burnings."

"What about the law that gives nesters the right to settle on land that hasn't been filed on?"

"All right," Daws countered. "What about it?"

"Y'mean the cattlemen wouldn't let it be enforced?"

"They would not."

"Ever think of getting a marshal to look into things around here?"

"We've done more than just think of it. We sent for one several times. When I saw you come down the street, I was sure you were the marshal. That's why I told you my name and asked if it meant anything to you. I sent out the appeals for help. So if you were the marshal, you'd have known my name."

"That feller they strung up today –"

"That was Ike Walters."

"What did he do?"

"Well, for one thing he was a homesteader."

"And for another?"

"He killed a cattleman. A miserable individual named Darrow. Seems he tried to drive a herd of steers shortcut over Walters' place and Walters protested. First they had words, then they went at each other with their fists. Darrow got the worst of the exchange, so he went for his gun. Apparently he wasn't any better with that than he was with his fists."

"Understand there's another hanging set for tomorrow."

"Yes. Ben Lundy."

"He a homesteader too?"

Daws nodded.

"And what did he do?"

"Tried to stop some cattlemen from burning him out. In the process he killed one of them."

"And so they're hanging him."

"Yes. But Walters and Lundy aren't the first to hang for defending themselves. There were others before them. Six to be exact, and all of them homesteaders."

"Sa-ay, there's a lunchroom somewhere down the street, isn't there?"

"A couple of doors from the corner," Daws answered. "On this side of the street."

"Gotta put something inside of me," Canavan said, hitching up his belt and pants. "My belly's empty and growling at me. So I'd better go do something about it. I'll see you again, Daws."

Daws did not answer. His expression reflected his disappointment when he poked his head out of the doorway and watched Canavan striding down the street.

"Maybe I was wrong about him," he thought to himself. "Maybe he isn't the kind we need in Paradise after all. He's big enough, but I guess that's all. Thought he might show more sympathy for Lundy than he did, maybe even want to do something to help him. That's why I told him as much as I did. But he didn't. He was more concerned with feeding himself. Guess I might as well acknowledge it. I've seen enough evidences of it to convince me. People are selfish and self-centered. The average individual won't willingly lift a finger to help the next fellow whose very life may depend upon others helping him save it."

It was after ten. Save for yellowish, almost brassy lamplight that sifted out through the saloon's open door and windows, the street was dark; except for the occasional outbursts of laughter from the saloon, it was hushed too. A tall, lean figure that was Canavan idled in the shadows in front of the hotel. Suddenly he moved, wheeled into the alley that flanked it and marched down its sloping length to the back yard. Rounding the building, he skidded into a rain barrel that refused to give way to him, and he cursed and backed off and hobbled about, rubbing his bruised knee. Finally, he circled wide around the barrel and went on. There were boxes and other things, including a discarded mattress, scattered about with what he now insisted was nothing short of deliberate and malicious carelessness. There were wash lines and line poles, and because of the obscuring darkness, each presented a hazard to him. Fortunately though, he managed to avoid any further mishaps; he seemed to sense when to stop and back off and circle around, and when to sidestep and go on. Soon he was past the hotel and threading his way through the littered yard of the next building. He passed through a third yard without incident, and then a fourth one, and then the sheriff's office was ahead of him.

He sidled up to the building that housed it, flattened himself out against the rear wall, and followed it inch by inch up to a barred and uncovered window through which thin lamplight rays were thrusting out and playing over the window sill and the ground below it. He stole a quick, cautious look inside. In the middle of the room there was a crude, makeshift table and a couple of chairs, one of which was pushed in close to it, the other half turned away from it. Beyond the table and against the wall was a cot on which a man lay sprawled out, half on his back, half on his side. The man stirred, swung his booted feet over the side of the cot, and sat up. But Canavan couldn't see his face; his hair was long and mussed and hung down over it. His shirt was torn, and one sleeve appeared to be hanging from it by a single thread. When he struggled to his feet and sought to stretch himself, Canavan saw that his wrists were lashed together behind him. Canavan's eyes shifted away from him and held for a moment on a closed door, the connecting door between the office proper and the back room, the latter the sheriff's living quarters and the detention room for lawbreakers awaiting trial, and in Ben Lundy's case, execution.

Bending low, Canavan crept past the window, and raising up again, glided past the back door and made his way farther downstreet to the saloon. The cellar door, he was agreeably surprised to find when he came up to it, was open, and he peered into the cellar hopefully. He could see turned-down lamplight playing over the planked floor. But he couldn't hear anyone moving about. Noiselessly, and with his hand on his gun butt, he went down the two, three, four steps, and halting in the open doorway, ranged a quick look around the place. There was no one there, no sign of anyone either. His eyes probed the far end of the cellar, searching the aisles between the neat, orderly floor-to-ceiling tiers of whiskey cases and the solid lines of sturdy beer kegs. After a bit he moved out of the doorway and halted again within touching distance of the lamp in its iron wall bracket, and stood for an uncertain moment within the circle of light that it cast off. When he spied a pile of strewn-about empty wooden cases and boxes, a heap of straw and some pieces of paper in a corner of the cellar, he crossed the floor eagerly, noticing then for the first time the thin hum of voices overhead, the thump of booted feet too. He produced a match, scratched it on his pants leg, and when it burst into flame, he jabbed it into the straw. It caught fire at once, and he wheeled around and darted up the stairs, closed the cellar door and bolted away.

Swiftly retracing his steps to the sheriff's office, he crouched down against the back wall and waited. The minutes passed slowly and he forced himself to bridle his impatience. Peering out anxiously, he saw smoke seeping out of the cellar through the unlocked door and decided he hadn't closed it very securely. More minutes passed, and suddenly there were yells from the direction of the saloon, and he knew that the flames had finally broken through the cellar ceiling and the saloon floor. Now the yells were louder and wilder, carrying through the brisk night air, and he looked up instantly when he heard a door close by open and slam. It was the street door to the sheriff's office, he told himself. Firing the saloon had accomplished its purpose; the yells had reached the sheriff who, apparently forgetting about his prisoner, had rushed out to find out what was going on.

Straightening up and backing off a couple of steps, Canavan yanked out his gun, pointed it at the lock on the back door and fired a bullet into it. Then gun in hand, he hurled himself at the door, twisting in mid-air in order to hit it with his hunched shoulder. The door gave way before him. He heard wood splinter, heard something strike the floor with a metallic ring to it and roll around. The impetus of his catapulting lunge carried him over the threshold in wild, careening flight. He stumbled and crashed heavily into the table, caromed off it and fell over a chair and went down with it.

II

Hastily, Canavan scrambled to his feet. The chair that he had fallen over lay on its side, nudging his right leg with one of its own. He reached for it and in almost the same motion slung it away. Then he lifted his eyes to the hair-mussed, wrist-bound man who was standing in front of his cot and staring at him.

"You Ben Lundy?" Canavan asked, hitching up his belt.

"Yes. But who are you?"

"You wouldn't know if I told you. Turn around." The homesteader did not move quickly enough to suit Canavan who spun him around and freed his hands. He jerked a spare gun out of his belt and handed it to Lundy. "That's for just-in-case. Let's go."

Then herding the homesteader doorward, he asked: "Where's your place?"

"About five miles north of here," Lundy answered over his shoulder.

"Maybe you'd better not go straight there. *They* will when they find you've broken out and they go looking for you. Circle around your place and hole up somewhere close by and stay put there till they get tired of looking and quit. Then get your family and clear out."

They emerged into the back yard.

"The way I went through here," Canavan said wryly as he pulled the door shut, "I was afraid I was gonna wind up on the far side of the office door too. Couldn't do anything about getting you a horse, Lundy, so you'll have to add horse stealing to your crimes. I spotted a couple tied up near the corner, so help yourself to one of them. Go 'head."

Lundy didn't move.

"Look, Mister," Canavan told him. "You're wasting valuable time standing here when you could be putting distance between you and –"

"That murdering little bastard Harp. I swore I'd kill him."

"Some other time, Lundy. Right now you've got other things to do. More important ones too. So get going, will you, before we both get caught?"

Lundy pushed past Canavan with such suddenness that he took Canavan by surprise; before thc latter could stop him, the homesteader had wheeled into the alley that flanked the sheriff's office. Canavan ran after him, overtook him, lunged and caught him by the arm, but before he could tighten his hold, Lundy broke away from him and bolted up the alley to the street. As Canavan reached the entrance to the alley and peered out he saw Lundy skid to a stop on the walk in front of the saloon, saw him stand in yellow lamplight that streamed out through the open door, and heard him holler:

"All right, Harp! Come out here, you murdering skunk, and get what's coming to you!"

"Oh, that damned fool!" Canavan muttered to himself. "I give him a chance to save his fool neck and he throws it away just like that!"

He saw Lundy back off the walk and step down into the gutter and halt again, still facing the saloon, with the gun that Canavan had given him leveled and holding on the doorway. There was no answer to his challenge. If Lundy had expected Harp to take it up, Canavan didn't. Harp couldn't be that much of a fool. He would answer, all right, but through someone else, someone who was better qualified to do it. A man in Harp's position would certainly have a couple of fast guns among his followers. He'd pick one of them and that would be it. Canavan peered out anxiously, fully aware of what was going to happen, yet hoping it wouldn't for Lundy's sake. To be saved from a noose only to tempt fate, even dare it to do its worst, made little sense to Canavan. However, it was his own life with which Lundy was being so reckless; if he didn't think any more of it than he appeared to, there wasn't anything anyone else could do to save it for him. As Canavan watched, Lundy backed off another step, then still another, and finally he was standing in the very middle of the gutter.

" 'S'matter, Harp, you bastard?" Canavan heard the homesteader yell tauntingly. "Haven't got the guts to come outside, have you?"

Suddenly there was a cry from Lundy; it sounded like a protest. His gun roared. But its voice, so loud and authoritative by itself, was lost, drowned out completely by an overpowering answering thunder of gunfire that was poured into him apparently from the alleyways on both sides of the saloon. Harp hadn't selected just one man to answer for him; he had delegated the duty to a handful of his followers. The hail of leaden slugs that slammed into Ben Lundy's body spun him around drunkenly, like a thin reed caught in a swirling storm. He staggered blindly, with one hand, his left, outthrust as though he were groping for something to cling to. His legs were buckling under him. A second blast of withering gunfire burst upon him, bracketing and riddling him, and he tottered brokenly, and toppled, dead before he struck the ground. Men spilled out of the alleys, four, five, six of them, with half raised guns in their hands. Canavan recognized one of them when he paused for a moment on the walk, on the very spot on which Lundy had stood. It was burly Mike Hoban. The other men followed him out to the gutter, to where Lundy lay in a slightly hunched-over heap. When a man with a lighted lantern swinging from his hand came trudging out from the saloon, someone pushed the fallen homesteader over on his back. Then with the lantern held above him, the men who had cut him down with their gunfire gathered a little closer around him and peered down at him. Now more men emerged from the saloon and joined the others; they too had a look at Lundy. Then slowly, Hoban first, then the other men, they holstered their guns and trooped back to the saloon at the heels of the man with the lantern. The street was hushed again, and the darkness seemed to deepen as it closed in around the dead man in the gutter as though it had already laid claim to him and was trying to shield him from prying eyes.

Since there was nothing to be gained and nothing more that he could do there save risk being detected, Canavan retreated down the alley, and retracing his steps through the littered yards, made his way back to the hotel. Fortunately there was no sign of the proprietor; there was instead an indication that he had already turned in. The dim light that had burned earlier in the tiny lobby had been lowered even more till now it was a bare flicker of light, just enough to point out the direction of the stairway. Canavan tiptoed up the stairs and slipped into his room and locked the door. He decided against striking a light, afraid that it might attract attention and arouse suspicion. He groped his way forward to the bed, hung his hat and gunbelt on the post, eased off his boots and slumped back across the bed. He was tired, but he knew there wouldn't be much sleep for him that night. Ben Lundy would see to that. Oh, why, Canavan demanded bitterly, had Lundy been such a fool? Why couldn't he have been satisfied with having been saved from hanging? Why hadn't he seen fit to take advantage of his unexpected freedom and use it to its fullest? He hadn't, and now he was dead, and Canavan felt bad about it, disappointed and angry too. He hadn't given any thought before to the fact that he had been risking his own neck in attempting to save Lundy's. Well, that wouldn't happen again, he told himself. In the future, he vowed, he would mind his own business, and he repeated it over and over again as he squared back. The moment he closed his eyes, Ben Lundy appeared. Canavan caught a glimpse of the hanged man, Walters, too, but Lundy insisted upon hogging the scene and crowded Walters out of it. After a while though, despite Lundy's dogged persistence, Canavan's tiredness overcame him and he drifted off to sleep.

It was dawn when he awoke. He sat up, pulled on his boots and hoisted himself up from the bed, went to the window and poked his head out. It was a gray, drab dawn with a touch of dampness in it. A chilling wind had come up and was spinning dust about aimlessly. Looking downstreet, Canavan saw three men lift Ben Lundy's riddled body onto a plank and trudge away with it. A fourth man, an aproned storekeeper, appeared carrying a too-well-filled bucket of water. He stopped instantly and glowered when some of the water spilled out and sloshed over his feet. Carrying the bucket a little more carefully, he stepped down into the gutter, splashed water over the reddish-brown spot where Lundy had died in his own blood, watched the water run over the mixture of blood and dirt, then tramped away.

Half an hour later when Canavan came downstairs the bald-headed hotel-keeper was behind the counter. He looked up, grunted and asked:

"Sleep all right?"

"Yeah, pretty good," Canavan told him.

Canavan, emerging from the hotel, strode downstreet. He slowed his step when he neared the boarded-up *Clarion* office, peered inside between two of the boards. There was no sign of anyone in the shadowy interior. He tried the door but it was locked; when there was no response to his knock, he went on again. Then as he came up to the saloon, Mike Hoban sauntered out.

"Morning, Mac," he said when he saw Canavan.

"Morning," Canavan acknowledged.

"Well?" Hoban asked, hitching up his pants and shifting his holster a little. "You make up your mind yet?"

"'Fraid not," Canavan said. "Musta dozed off sooner than I expected to last night, and instead of sleeping on the idea and wakin' up with an answer, I spent the whole blamed night dreaming about a lot of good things to eat."

Hoban's thick lips parted in a grin.

"Sure it wasn't about the woman who was gonna do the cookin'?" he asked slyly.

"I know damned well it wasn't," Canavan retorted, "because I didn't see any woman in the dream and when I woke up, I was so blamed starved, you'da thought I hadn't had anything to eat for a week. If that lunchroom down the street is open . . ."

"Gener'lly opens around six."

"It's nearly seven now."

"Then it oughta be open."

"Then that's where I'm heading. I'm gonna pack away a man-sized breakfast, believe me. The works."

Hoban rubbed his bristly chin with the back of his big, thick hand.

"Think I'll go along with you, Mac," he said after a moment's thought. "Listening to you, I've suddenly come up with an appetite. Although that lunchroom isn't exactly the place when you've got a hankering for some really good grub. And that sign he has in the window that says 'Home Cooking' is a lie."

"Any place else where we can eat?"

Hoban shook his head.

"Nope," he replied.

"Then it looks like we haven't any choice in the matter."

Together they walked down the street. Hoban lifted his gaze skyward for a moment and remarked:

"Looks like it might be trying to clear."

Canavan looked skyward too.

"Yeah," he agreed and added: "If the sun would come out and burn off the dampness..."

"Yeah," Hoban said, "If."

"Say, Mike, meant to ask you this right off. Did I hear some gunplay last night, or was that something else I dreamed up?"

"Oh, it was gunplay, all right," Hoban answered grimly. Canavan, stealing a look at him, saw his beady eyes burn. "We had a hanging set for this morning. A no-good, murdering nester named Lundy. Seems he broke outta the sheriff's back room some time last night. But instead of hightailing it while he had the chance, the damned fool decided he'd try a little shoot-out with us. We blasted him good."

"H'm," Canavan said with a shake of his head. "He musta been out've his mind to try anything like that."

"He musta been outta something," big Hoban said.

"Saved you the trouble of stringin' him up."

"That's right. Now I'd like to get my hands on the one who helped him break out."

"Got any idea who it mighta been?"

"I don't think it was anybody from town. I think it was another nester. They stick together, you know."

"Uh-huh."

"But we'll catch up with him one o' these days," Hoban continued, and his eyes glinted again. "Somebody'll talk outta turn and give him away and we'll hear about it and grab him. And when we bring him in, that'll be that. We'll hang him higher'n a kite. You aimin' to head out today, Mac?"

"No-o, I think I'll stay around for another day or two."

"That's good," Hoban said, nodding.

"After I've put something away inside of me," Canavan went on, "I think I'll go saddle up that mare of mine and run her a little. Stopped in at the stable when I came out of the hotel and looked in on her. She was stamping and fussin' around like a good feller. Think I'd better get her out of there before she gets a mad on and kicks down the stall."

Hoban grinned.

"Or she takes into her fool head to go after Lindfors, the stableman, and kick his head off. Oh, here we are, Mac. Here's where we get some home cooking, Paradise style."

He led the way into the lunchroom.

It was about an hour later, just about eight-fifteen, when Canavan wheeled Aggie out of the stable and rode down the street. The mare snorted and pranced and Canavan had to speak sharply to her a couple of times. There were a couple of men idling in front of the saloon, Hoban among them, when Canavan rode up. Hoban gave him a half-salute and called: "Frisky as all get-out, Mac, ain't she?"

"She was about set to kick the stable apart when I went in to get her," Canavan related.

Hoban crossed the walk to the curb, and Canavan pulled up.

"Give her her head when you get her out in the open," the former advised. "Run her till her tongue hangs out, then wallop her good a couple of times. Maybe that'll take some of the temper out've her."

Canavan nodded, settled himself a little more comfortably in the saddle, eased his grip on the reins and the mare loped away. Quickening her pace as she swept down the street, she took the upgrade in full stride. Topping it, her flashing hoofs drummed a swift beat westward. Half a mile, then a mile, and Canavan, after twisting around and taking a quick look behind him to make certain that he wasn't being trailed, swung Aggie northward. It was only then that he became aware of the clearing, brightening sky, noticed too the lifting rich goodness of the lush, dew-wet grass. Another mile and they passed a herd of grazing steers. Some of the animals wheeled after them; they were outdistanced so quickly, they pulled up almost at once, turned around and plodded back and rejoined their mates. More miles slipped away behind Canavan as the fleet-footed mare maintained her fast pace. Then about half a mile off in the distance Canavan spotted a cabin with a field of towering wheat behind it.

They came sweeping up to the cabin shortly. Canavan reined in and sat back in the saddle, ranging his gaze critically over the crudely fashioned structure. It was weather-beaten and drab-looking, and save for its gleaming, curtained window, it looked abandoned. There was a lean-to diagonally beyond it, with a canvas drop-curtain hanging crookedly over its entrance. There was no sign though, no sound either, of a horse behind the curtain. A heavy farm wagon stood close by, one corner of it resting on a wooden block since it had only three wheels. The fourth one, with a couple of its thick spokes broken and others missing entirely, lay near it on the trampled ground. The iron rim had been pried off the wheel and was propped up against the wagon. Canavan swung down off Aggie's back, walked to the door and knocked on it. There was no response; he knocked a second time. When there was no answer, he stepped back; rounding the cabin to the rear, he had to side-step alertly to avoid colliding with a wash-line post. The line itself was bare. But nearby, atop an upended wooden box was a basket half-filled with wrung out wash. There was no back door to the cabin, hence he retraced his steps to the front door. This time he didn't knock; he tried the door. He was a little surprised when it opened. He pushed it open wide and stopped as he was about to cross the threshold strip. Sitting head-bowed and hunched-over at the table that stood squarely in the middle of the bare cabin floor was a woman. Her hands hung limply at her sides.

"Oh," Canavan said. "Excuse me."

Slowly she raised her head, turned a red-eyed, tear-stained face in his direction. It was a pretty face, and a surprisingly young one.

"You Mrs. Lundy?" he asked.

"Yes," she answered dully.

"Like to talk to you about your husband. All right if I come in?"

"Ben's dead," she said, again in the same flat, dull tone.

"Oh, then you know!"

"Yes," she said heavily. "I know. I was just about to hang the wash when they came and told me."

He took off his hat as he stepped inside, moved around the table and stopped across from where she sat. Her eyes held on him.

"Sit down," she said with an off-handed gesture.

He drew a chair back from the table and seated himself.

"Thought I was doing him a good turn," he said with an unhappy shake of his head, "helping him break out of the sheriff's office. Only it didn't work out that way."

Her mouth opened and she stared at him.

"Instead of getting away from there while he had the chance," he continued, "he wouldn't go, insisted he was going to get Judge Harp first. I tried to stop him, to talk some sense into him, but it wasn't any use. When he ran out to the street and hollered to Harp to come outside, Harp's men shot him down."

"So that's what happened!" she said. Her mouth tightened and an angry light burned in her eyes. "Then if you had minded your own business, he'd still be alive." Then she raged: "Why did you have to butt in? Why couldn't you have –"

"Mrs. Lundy," he interrupted. "I don't know for sure if you know this, but they were going to hang your husband this morning."

"Of course I knew that!" she flung at him. "But something inside of me kept telling me all along they wouldn't hang him. That at the last minute they'd let him go."

"But they hung those other nesters," he pointed out. "Last one was yesterday. That Ike Walters. Then what could've made you think they'd go easy on your husband and let him off?"

"I just told you," she retorted. "That . . . that feeling I had that they wouldn't hang Ben."

He made no reply.

"That's why I didn't go to town this morning," she went on. "I was so sure he'd be coming home."

"H'm," Canavan said.

"But now he's dead and I'm all alone."

"No family, Mrs. Lundy? No folks anywhere, and no friends?"

"I haven't anyone."

"What about your husband? Didn't he have any folks either?"

"No," she answered with a shake of her head. Her eyes suddenly blazed again. "All I know is that my husband would still be alive if it hadn't been for you. You're just as much to blame for what happened to him, we-ll, as those men are, the ones who did the actual killing. Now what are you going to do about it?"

He was a little taken aback by the bluntness of her question. "Don't think there's anything much I can do about it," he said.

"Oh, you don't! Well, you'd better think again and real hard too. You're responsible for Ben's death and no one's going to make me think different. And now that he's gone and I haven't anyone else, that makes you responsible for me. For what happens to me."

"Now just a minute, Mrs. Lundy," he said. "I never laid eyes on your husband before last night, and I never saw you before till just a minute ago. If you think you're gonna sucker me into takin' the blame for your husband getting himself killed and then try to saddle me with you, you've got another think coming."

He got to his feet, clapped his hat on his head, yanked down the brim and hitched up his pants. Tears filled her eyes and coursed down her cheeks. He looked at her and frowned.

"All right," she said with an empty, helpless gesture of her hands. "There isn't any food here and I haven't any money to buy any with. And I can't stay here. But if you haven't any sense of decency or responsibility . . ."

Her voice trailed away. She began to sob. His frown deepened. He dug in his pocket and produced a handful of silver and a couple of wadded-up bills. He returned the silver to his pocket, smoothed out the bills and tossed them on the table.

"Here," he said curtly. He pushed the money across the table. "Any way for you to get to town?"

"Oh, I'll get there all right."

"Got a horse somewhere around?"

"An old one, yes."

"Where've you got him?"

"Behind the lean-to," she answered.

"Well, get yourself to town," he instructed her, "and find yourself a place to live. There are a couple of decent enough boarding houses to choose from. When you get yourself set, leave word for me at the hotel so I'll know you're all right."

"I don't even know your name."

"It's Canavan."

"Canavan?" she repeated. She dabbed at her moist eyes with her handkerchief and dried them.

"C-a-n-a-v-a-n. Now look, lady. I'm willing to help you get yourself settled somewhere. I'll even help you while you're getting yourself something to do. But once you do, that'll be it. As far as I'll go along with this thing. That clear?"

She made no response.

"Now here's something else. If Harp and his outfit find out it was me who helped Ben make his break, my life won't be worth much. Aside from me, you're the only one who knows I had a hand in it. I want it to stay that way. Nobody else has to know. Leastways not till it doesn't matter any more. Understand?"

She nodded, arose and followed him when he went to the door. When he stepped outside, she stood in the doorway, watched him climb up on Aggie's back, followed him with her eyes when he rode away. And when he was out of sight, she closed the door.

Crossing the street after he had returned an apparently more contented Aggie to her stall, Canavan stopped when he came to the *Clarion* office and peered in through the open door. Daws was sitting at his desk, thumbing through some papers. Canavan walked in, closed the door behind him, and Daws promptly twisted around and looked up.

"Oh," he said when he saw Canavan.

"Got a back room where we can talk?"

"Yes," Daws answered, and he looked a little oddly at him, Canavan thought. "This way."

The stocky man led the way to the rear, through a curtained doorway and into a small, almost square room through whose uncovered window Canavan glimpsed the back yard. Shelves lined the white-washed walls. On them were stacks of folded newspapers, books, boxes, bottles of ink and other things. There were two wooden boxes standing in a corner, one on top of the other; Daws brought them forward, upended them, seated himself on one and when Canavan sat down on the other, he asked: "What would you like to talk about?"

"How 'bout Ben Lundy?"

"He's dead."

"I know. I wasn't going to tell you this, Daws. Leastways not just yet a while. But I guess you might as well know it. Lundy didn't break out of the sheriff's office by himself."

"I didn't think he did," was the calm reply. "I knew he must have had help from someone on the outside."

"I was the one on the outside."

Daws' eyebrows arched the barest bit, but that was all.

"Want to tell me about it?"

"Yeah, sure." Canavan related the story of Ben Lundy's brief taste of freedom. The newspaper publisher listened without comment or interruption. "That's it as far as Lundy was concerned. Now I want to tell you about his wife." That part of Canavan's recital consumed more minutes. Finally, finished, he sat back on his box. "How do you like that?"

"I think the best comment I can offer at this point, Canavan, is simply that men think one way, women another. Sometimes, listening to some women air their viewpoints, I'm absolutely at a loss for words. How their minds function, and how they arrive at some conclusions, we-ll, just about staggers me. Lundy's wife and her unreasonable attitude proves that, doesn't it?"

"Yeah, pretty much. But you watch how fast I unload her the minute I think she oughta be able to take care of herself."

Daws nodded and said: "You know, Canavan, you beat us, four of Lundy's homesteader neighbors and me, to getting him out of custody by a matter of minutes."

"That so?" Canavan smiled wryly. "Too bad for me I didn't hold off making my move till later on. Then I would've been out of it altogether."

"The four of them slipped into town under

cover of darkness," Daws continued, "and waited with me right in this very room till we thought it was time for us to strike. Just as we were about to set out for the sheriff's office, we heard yelling outside. The men waited while I hurried off to find out what had happened. When I found that the saloon cellar was on fire, I decided that that was the opportune moment for us. I rushed back and got the others. When we got to the sheriff's office and found Lundy gone, we knew what had happened. That the fire had been started to cover up Lundy's jailbreak, to attract everyone's attention away from where he was being held. We came back here wondering what to do. When we heard the shooting downstreet, I went out to investigate. I saw Harp's men swarm out of the alleys after shooting down Lundy."

"How'd you know it was him?"

"I heard one of them say he'd saved them the trouble of hanging him."

"Oh!"

"So there wasn't any question in my mind as to the identity of the dead man whom they'd left lying in the street."

"If you hadda headed for the sheriff's place through the yards instead of going down the street, chances are we'd have run into each other. Oh, Lundy's wife said something about 'them' stopping and telling her about Lundy. The 'them' she was talking about the same four nesters you were talking about?"

"Yes. When they left here they told me they would stop at the Lundy place and let Mrs. Lundy know what had happened."

Canavan climbed to his feet.

"What now, my friend?" Daws asked.

"Don't know yet," Canavan replied. "Got a couple of ideas on how to hit back at Harp kickin' around in here," and he tapped his head with his finger. "Want to think about them a while longer. When I figure out which one is the best for us to play along with, I'll let you know."

Daws stood up too.

"What about California?" he asked with a smile.

"California?" Canavan repeated. "It's been where it is for a long, long time. I think it will still be there when I finally get around to heading out there. So long for now, Daws."

III

It was probably an hour later. Canavan lay slumped across his bed, staring up at the cracked ceiling. When he heard heavy bootsteps on the stairs, he raised his head and listened; when they came closer, he forced himself up into a sitting position. He had just gotten to his feet when the bootsteps came up to his door. There was a heavy-handed thump on the door; before he could answer, the door opened and Mike Hoban poked his head in.

"Hi, Mac," he said.

"Oh, hello, Mike," Canavan responded. "Come in."

Hoban stepped inside, stopped and closed the door, and sauntered forward. He halted again abreast of the bureau and, standing spread-legged with his thumbs hooked in his belt, rocked a little on his heels.

"Didn't know if you'd come back yet," he said. Then with a thin smile parting his lips, he asked: "That mare o' yours get it through her head that you won't stand for her acting up?"

"Yeah, I think so," Canavan replied. "But for how long she'll remember it, I don't know. I'll probably have to remind her of it every once in a while. What's on your mind?"

Hoban eased his hat up from his forehead and let it ride on the back of his head. Again red, angry-looking lines curved around his temples, and he rubbed them with the backs of his hands.

"Damned hat's too tight on me," he said, frowning. "Took it off a nester we were stringin' up because mine was old and just about shot. Shoulda known better though. Anything you ever get off a nester isn't worth taking."

Canavan held his tongue, waited instead for him to go on.

"Been talking to the boss about you, Mac," Hoban said shortly. He stopped rubbing his temples. The angry lines had gone. However, now his forehead from one side to the other was reddened. "Gave him quite a spiel about you."

"Oh?"

"Said he'd like to meet you. Told me to bring you back with me so we could sit down and have a drink together and get to know each other."

"Thanks, Mike, but there wouldn't be any point to it."

"Mean you've made up your mind? It's still California?"

"That's right," Canavan said, nodding.

"Sorry to hear that," Hoban said, and he looked genuinely disappointed. He managed a wry smile and said: "Kinda hoped you'd decide to stay on here and tie up with us. You and me, we'da made a helluva pair."

"Yeah," Canavan acknowledged. "Guess we would have at that. But..."

He didn't finish. His hands and shoulders lifted in an empty shrug.

Hoban straightened up. He settled his hat firmly on his head, tugged at the brim a couple of times, frowned when it refused to go down any further, and said: "Stop by anyway and lemme buy you a drink."

Canavan grinned. "That's what I'm afraid of. That's why I haven't stopped by up to now."

"How d'you mean you're afraid?"

"Oh, you'll trot out some real good stuff and kinda mellow me and the first thing I know you'll sweet-talk me into staying on." Canavan grinned again. "So I think I'll steer clear of you and your liquor, Mike. That way I'll stand a better chance of getting to California before I get too old to care where I go."

Hoban laughed.

"All the same, I'm not giving up on you," he said as he turned and walked doorward.

He opened the door and looked back at Canavan and said: "Not till I know for sure that you've gone."

The door closed after him. Canavan heard him go down the stairs, then he backed to the bed and slumped down again across it. His eyes closed and he dozed off. A rough hand shook him into awakening. He experienced some little difficulty getting his sleep-laden eyes properly focused, then he saw that it was Mike Hoban, strangely grim-faced this time, who was bending over him.

"Oh," he said, struggling into a sitting position. "It's you, Mike. Closed my eyes and musta dozed off for a minute."

"That was some minute," Hoban retorted. "More like two hours. You'd better get going, Mac."

"Huh?"

"While the going's still good," Hoban added.

"What's the idea?"

"I told you somebody would spill his guts and we'd find out who it was that helped that Lundy polecat break out've the sheriff's place, didn't I?"

"Yeah. But what's that got to do with me? Oh, I see! You think it was me. Is that it?"

"We don't think it, Mac," Hoban said quietly. "We know."

Their eyes met and held for a moment. Then Hoban stepped back and came erect. Canavan climbed to his feet. As Hoban watched, Canavan smoothed back his hair with his hands, pushed his shirttail deeper down inside his pants.

"I'll probably be sorry for this," Hoban went on. "But I kinda took a shine to you, Mac. That is, Canavan. That's why I'm giving you a chance to get your horse, saddle her up and get going away from here before the judge sends some of the boys around to pay you off for horning in something that wasn't any of your business."

"Sorry you bothered, Mike."

"You'll be a helluva lot sorrier if you don't get a move on."

"I'm staying put, Mike," Canavan said quietly. "I'm not leaving Paradise just yet."

Hoban leveled a frowning look at him.

"Oh," he said. "So that's how it's gonna be! First it was that damned mare of yours acting up. Now it's you."

"No," Canavan said with a shake of his head. "I'm not acting up. I'm just telling you."

"I've played fair with you, Canavan. Play the same way with me."

"All right. What do you want to know?"

"Just one thing. You a lawman?"

"Nope."

"Then what in blazes made you help that nester break out?"

"I didn't think he'd had a fair chance, and I wanted him to have one."

"H'm," Hoban said darkly. "You know how long you'll stay alive buckin' us, don't you?"

"The odds don't worry me."

"They'd better," Hoban said grimly. "We've got a dozen men who can sling a gun with the best."

"I've tangled with some of the best in my time, Mike."

"Then there's just this much more, Canavan. I'm tied up with the judge. Now you oughta be able to figure out for yourself what that's gonna mean far as you and me are concerned."

"It probably means that we'll wind up gunning for each other," Canavan replied.

"That's right. But that's the way you want it. Right?"

Canavan didn't answer.

Hoban looked hard at him, hitched up his pants rather viciously, wheeled around and stalked out of the room. Canavan stood motionlessly for perhaps a minute, then he caught up his hat, clapped it on his head and went out too. When he emerged into the street, he saw Hoban some thirty feet away striding off in the direction of the saloon. He waited till he saw the burly man slant across the walk as he neared the saloon and go inside. Then Canavan marched down the street too and turned in at the *Clarion* office. Daws came out of the back room as Canavan entered. The newspaper editor eyed him questioningly.

"Harp knows," Canavan announced, and Daws looked up at him blankly. "That it was me," Canavan explained, "who helped Lundy break out."

"Oh," Daws said, and he looked concerned. "Then you'd better get out of town and in a hurry too."

"No," Canavan said. "I'm not doing anything of the kind. I'm staying put. Look, Daws, you have any influence with the storekeepers in town?"

"Some, I suppose. But why do you ask? What've you got in mind?"

"Harp's bleeding them white, isn't he? Making them pay through the nose in taxes?"

"Yes. And in view of the excessive amounts he's levied on them, I find it hard to understand how most of them manage to meet his demands and still pay their bills. They're probably having to draw on what little they've managed to save over the years they've been in business."

"However they're doing it doesn't matter right now. What might matter is this. If they were to close up shop and clear out, for the time being that is, till we get rid of Harp and his crew, he wouldn't have any income, would he?"

"No."

"Then he'd have to look elsewhere for another place for himself, right? For another town to move in on and take over?"

"Right."

"But maybe by then the law will have caught up with him and he won't get a chance to go looking for anything."

"I'd like to see that happen."

"So would I. And maybe we will see it happen. Meanwhile though, would you like to see what you can do with the storekeepers?"

"When? Oh, you mean right now?"

"Got anything more important to do?"

"No-o. I was just transferring some things to the back room. But I can go on with that later on." Daws stood thoughtfully silent for a moment, then he said: "Don't expect too much right off, Canavan. A few of the storekeepers, those with more courage than the others, who'd welcome any opportunity to hit back at Harp, they'll take the lead and close up without too much delay. Some of the others, the more cautious ones, will want to think about it before they commit themselves. The rest who knuckle down to anyone who comes along will want to see how things go for those who close up before they do anything themselves."

"Uh-huh," Canavan said. "If we could get half of them to close up, the others will soon find themselves over a barrel, won't they, because Harp will try to force them to make up the difference to him? In other words, Daws, a storekeeper who's been paying say ten bucks a week is liable to find himself having to pay say twenty, or maybe even twenty-five a week."

"There isn't a storekeeper in Paradise who will be able to meet that demand and still stay in business," Daws said firmly.

"Good," Canavan acknowledged. "Then the sooner we get things started around here, the sooner we'll be able to see results. I'm kinda curious to see what Harp will do when his hand is forced."

"Today's Wednesday, isn't it?"

"It figures," Canavan answered with a grin, "being that it was Tuesday yesterday. But what's that got to do with . . . ?"

"Wednesday is collection day for Harp."

"Oh, I see!"

"His man usually makes the rounds some time in the afternoon."

"Uh-huh," Canavan said again. "Think any of the storekeepers might refuse to kick in this time after you get finished talking to them?"

Daws shook his head.

"No," he said flatly. "A couple of them tried to stand up to Harp in the beginning. A good beating and they quickly fell into line. No one's tried it since."

"Don't blame them," Canavan commented wryly. "A busted skull can be awfully discouraging."

"How do you think Harp found out about you?"

"How d'you think he did?" Canavan countered.

"From Mrs. Lundy?"

"It figures, doesn't it? Only ones who knew were you two. And somehow I don't think it was you who blabbed to Harp."

"Believe me, I wasn't the one."

"Want to know something, Daws? I don't think you did either."

"Thank you. However, if you're as smart as I think you are, Canavan, after you told her, you must have had some misgivings about her. You did, didn't you?"

" 'Course," Canavan answered. "But once

I'd told her, there wasn't anything I could do 'cept hope she'd keep her mouth shut. But I'm willing to admit I didn't expect her to spill what she knew so soon. But now that it's out, maybe it's just as well."

"I'm afraid I don't see it quite that way."

"Well, for one thing, that lets me off the hook far as she's concerned. Now she can shift for herself and whatever she does won't be any skin offa my nose."

"Go on."

"For another thing," Canavan continued, "now that Harp's found out, maybe it will mean a showdown. If we're lucky, we'll win out. If we aren't lucky, we'll at least throw a scare into Harp, and if it's enough of one, he's liable to read the handwriting on the wall and decide not to push his luck here any longer, and clear out. So either way, we stand to win."

"I see," Daws said a little thoughtfully.

Canavan smiled grimly and added: " 'Course there's only one rub, and that's if our luck runs out on us."

"You mean we won't be alive to celebrate whatever we may have won?"

"That's the general idea, Daws. But don't let's look at the dark side till we have to. There's always time enough for that. All right?"

"I don't give up too easily."

"I don't either, Daws. Maybe that's why I'm still alive today. I've been jumped, slugged, knifed and shot. But instead of quitting after each one, I stuck around. Must've proved discouraging to the ones who were out to get me because the first thing I knew they were the ones who pulled in their horns and hightailed it. See you later."

It was shortly after seven o'clock when Canavan entered the lunchroom, perched himself on a stool and hunched over the counter on his folded arms. Mailler, the proprietor of the place, pushed out through the swinging half-door that led to the kitchen and, wiping his hands on his apron, moved behind the counter and asked: "What do you want to eat, Mister?"

Canavan lifted his eyes to him.

"What've you got?"

"Beef stew's the special for today. The kind your mother used to fix."

"Not my mother," Canavan answered with a shake of his head. "None of us liked it, so she never fixed it. Got any meat in your stew?"

Mailler's eyes opened wide and his jaw unhinged itself and hung.

"Got any meat in it?" he repeated in

shocked tones. "Now who ever heard of makin' beef stew without any meat in it?"

"I did," Canavan said calmly. "What's more, I've eaten it. That's how I found out there wasn't any meat in it. Just potatoes, a handful of chopped carrots and some other stuff, and a thick gravy."

"Huh," Mailler scoffed. He retraced his steps to the kitchen. When he returned a couple of minutes later, he placed a steaming, heaped-up plate in front of Canavan, followed it with a smaller plate of biscuits, butter, a knife, fork and spoon. Then with his arms folded over his flat chest, he said: "All right, Mister. Dig in. I want to hear what you have to say after you've eaten some of my stew."

He watched, peering hard, head thrust forward, as Canavan mouthed and ate his first forkful.

"Well?" he asked impatiently when Canavan made no comment but took a second forkful.

"It's doggoned hot," Canavan told him, shifting himself a little on his stool.

"What do you want? Cold stew? Now what about the meat?"

"I don't know. I swallowed something that felt a little lumpy. But it was too hot for me to tell what it was. You think that might have been the meat?"

Mailler frowned.

"Not all the meat, Mister," he said stiffly. "Just one piece of it."

He looked hurt. He gave Canavan an indignant stare and stalked back to the kitchen. The half-door swung behind him and thumped a couple of times, and finally hung motionlessly. After some minutes had gone by, the door creaked a little and Mailler poked his head out and stole a look at Canavan. But he couldn't tell anything, so still disappointed, he withdrew his head. But then when Canavan finished eating the stew, raised his head as he squared back on his stool and called, "Hey, partner!" Mailler poked his head out again.

"Got to hand it to you. That was real good," Canavan said.

Mailler's face brightened. He even managed a toothy smile.

"Coffee," Canavan ordered. "And what've you got to go with it?"

"Apple pie and chocolate cake," was the prompt reply.

"I'll take the chocolate cake," Canavan said after a moment's consideration. "And make it a good-sized chunk while you're at it."

"Right, mister."

Mailler brought him a generous-sized cut of the cake and a cup of coffee. He put them down on the counter and turned away; he stopped, seemed to be debating something with himself, then he retraced his steps and stood again in front of Canavan. The latter lifted his eyes to him, looked at him wonderingly. Mailler's face had suddenly paled.

"What's the matter with you?" Canavan asked. "You sick or something, or did you suddenly see a ghost?"

"Mister," Mailler said. "I should have told you this before. Only I forgot till just now. This afternoon a couple of the judge's hands stopped by here, said they were looking for a big, red-headed feller and they wanted to know if you, if he, eats here."

"Oh?"

"Can't remember what name they said though."

"Was it Canavan?"

"Yeah," Mailler said instantly. "That's it. That'd be you, wouldn't it, Mister? The description sure fits you and you knew the name. You ... you have some trouble with them?"

"No, but I think they're spoiling for some. Those two men, partner, what did they look like?"

"One of them was Marve Russell. He comes from around this way. Kinda husky-built and round-faced."

"And light-haired?"

"That's right. That's Marve, all right."

"What about the other one?" Canavan wanted to know. "Dark, wiry, thin-faced, with quick, nervous eyes?"

"Uh-huh," Mailler said nodding. "His name's Vasco. Leastways that's what I think it was that Marve called him."

"I know them," Canavan said. "I know who they are."

"That Marve doesn't look like the kind, but he's sure got himself a nasty temper. Flies off the handle just like that," Mailler said, snapping his fingers. "And that other one, that Vasco feller, I wouldn't want any part of him either. No, sir. Not me. He's got a mean, ornery look."

He stole a quick, side-long glance doorward. Canavan noticed it and asked: "What's the matter now?"

"Thought that was them when I was bringing you the cake," Mailler answered low-toned, out of a corner of his mouth. "But I wasn't sure because they were standing back in a doorway. So I just took another look. It's them, all right. Only now there's a third one with them."

"What are they doing?"

"Just standing across the street and looking over here. Oh, they've come out to the curb." Then excitedly: "They're coming across, Mister."

"Get outta here," Canavan ordered.

"You think there'll be shooting?"

" 'Fraid so. Got a back door to this place? Then use it, partner, and now."

Mailler needed no urging. He stepped back from the counter, suddenly wheeled around and fled. The half-door swung wildly behind him and thumped a couple of times, then another door, this one somewhere at the rear, slammed. Canavan eased himself around on his stool, and slowly, almost deliberately so, got up on his feet and stood facing the open door. Vasco and Russell were stepping up on the walk. His gaze ranged past them for an instant, seeking the third man. He spied him at once. He had stepped down into the gutter, and now he was stepping back on the opposite curb. Canavan moved backward unhurriedly between the stool on which he had been sitting and the one next to it, and rested his elbows on the edge of the counter, with the fingers of his right hand flexing and half closing, then opening again partially in crab-like fashion above the butt of his gun.

Vasco came in first. No sign of recognition passed between him and Canavan. His face seemed thinner and darker than Canavan remembered it, and his darting eyes, sweeping the lunchroom, were harder and a little narrowed. Shifting his holster a bit, Vasco sauntered past Canavan and eased himself down on a stool at the far end of the counter. Then Russell, hitching up his levis, swaggered inside, glowered a little at Canavan, and passed him. When Vasco pointed, Russell stopped at a side-wall table, spun a chair around and straddled it, and sitting slightly hunched forward in it, lifted his eyes to Canavan. The third man came in too. He looked a little hesitant, as though he weren't completely certain as to what he was supposed to do. When Vasco waved him back, he actually looked relieved, and hastily backed out and took up his position outside the door. Then slowly he began to back out to the curb. He would be out of the fight, Canavan told himself. Apparently his job was to guard the door in case Canavan sought to break out of the place. Canavan shifted his gaze back to Vasco and Russell.

"All right, Marve!" Vasco suddenly yelled.

He leaped off his stool with his right hand streaking holsterward, while Russell came to his feet clumsily, clawing for his gun. There was a thunderous deafening clap of gunfire. The lunchroom seemed to rock and the dishes on the wall shelves rattled. The front windowpane fell out with a shattering crash.

Gunfire drummed again, briefly though, and ceasing, left the air throbbing with gently lifting and fading echoes.

Marve Russell, his full face an expressionless blank, was sitting on the floor with his overturned chair lying across his legs. There was a strange limpness about him. His thick-wristed hands were down, resting on the floor at his sides, even his right hand in which his gun was still gripped. He raised his left hand and brushed the hat off his head. It fluttered backward and dropped to the floor. His head began to bow. There was blood on his shirtfront, a smear of it, just above the second button; fresh blood, surging from a second wound, this one also in his chest but more toward his shoulder, began to spread and deepen across the front of him. Suddenly he sagged and toppled sideways to the floor, his head thumping on it dully. His right hand opened and his gun slid out of it.

At the far end of the counter, Vasco was on his feet, his legs wide-spread to support his quivering body. He was clutching his wrist, his right one, with his left hand, trying to stop the spurting flow of blood from his shattered wrist. The blood gushed too freely and seeped through his fingers and ran down his pants leg and on to his boots and slithered off it to the floor, barely missing his gun which lay but an inch or two beyond it.

Canavan, with his gun still leveled, and a tiny wisp of blue smoke curling gently about him, was slowly rising from a half crouch on the table side of the lunchroom. He came erect shortly and looked critically at Vasco, then at the hunched-over body of Marve Russell. There was scorn in the look he gave them. Vasco, his eyes smouldering and his thin lips curled, glared at him, but Canavan disregarded him. Apparently satisfied that he had nothing further to fear from the inept Vasco, he lowered his gun. He kicked Vasco's across the floor, heard it strike and carom off the wall, spin and collide with a chair or table leg and stop its flight; he lashed out with his foot at Russell's gun and sent it spinning away too. Suddenly remembering that there was still the third man to be dealt with, he wheeled around to the doorway.

The shattering windowpane, spewing broken glass and littering the walk, had forced the man to retreat again into the gutter. That was where he was standing now, almost backed against the far-side curb, with his gun in his hand. Behind him on the narrow walk were townsmen and shopkeepers, out of breath, wide-eyed and excited-looking men. Canavan stepped into the doorway. Instantly the onlookers began to back away, crowding and trampling one another in their haste to get out of gun range. The third man shot a frantic and appealing look over his shoulder, but no one came to his side. All he could hear behind him was the sound of retreating and scurrying boots. Then, realizing that he had been left alone to face Canavan, his face whitened, and his eyes, nervous and darting, betrayed him and revealed his fear. Probing behind him with his foot, he found the curbing and quickly stepped up on the walk as Canavan, with his gun half-raised, emerged from the lunchroom, and crunching broken bits of glass underfoot, sauntered across the walk to the curb and stepped down into the gutter. The white-faced man began to edge away. His gun wavered a bit in his unsteady hand. He half turned away from Canavan, and the latter, watching him alertly, thought he was going to run. But he didn't. For a long, tensed, hushed moment he was motionless, as though fear had rooted him to the spot and was holding him frozen in its grip. Then slowly he turned around again, his shoulders lifting and squaring as he faced Canavan. Suddenly he flung a shot at Canavan and bolted away. Instinctively Canavan's gun snapped upward for an answering shot, and leveled. The target was one that he couldn't miss. But he did not shoot. He couldn't. The fleeing man was such a pathetically frightened creature, Canavan couldn't help but feel sorry for him. His lip curled a little though as he watched the man race up the street; when he saw him swerve and dart into the saloon, Canavan shook his head.

"Just about scared out of his wits," he muttered. "Bet he'll never be the same again, not even if he lives to be a hundred."

Slowly he straightened up, reloaded his gun and shoved it down into his holster. He backed to the curb and stepped up on it. There was a rush of booted feet as men burst out of their places of safety, now that the shooting appeared to be over, and converged upon the scene. Some of them, apparently those who were always attracted to any scene of excitement, but who were a little squeamish and couldn't bring themselves to venture too close to either a killing or spilled blood, halted on the opposite walk. The others, those for whom bloodshed and violent death seemed to hold some sort of morbid fascination, came scurrying across the street. They glanced at Canavan as they mounted the curb, but hastily averted their gaze when his hard eyes met theirs. They surged past him and crowded around the doorway of the lunchroom and peered in.

Canavan, backing across the walk, watched

them. A path opened at once when Vasco came stumbling out to the door. He was still clutching his shattered wrist, and blood was still dripping from it. There were bloodstains on his right pants leg, but they were brownish now rather than crimson. He glared into the sea of faces that stared at him, and he stepped outside, and trailing blood, plodded away up the street. The path that had opened for him closed again, and men crowded doorward a second time. Some of them pushed into the lunchroom and bent over Russell.

"He hit bad?" Canavan heard one onlooker ask from the doorway.

"Looks like it," someone answered.

"He's dead," another voice said flatly.

More men shouldered their way into the lunchroom.

"Watch it there, you fellers. Watch it," a grumpy voice said. "You're standin' right in his blood, Jess."

Canavan was suddenly aware of a pair of appraising eyes on him. He looked across the street. Looking at him with unconcealed interest was a man who was standing alone, apart from the others, on the opposite side. Canavan found himself studying the man with equal interest. About average in height, rather slender in build, he wore tailored clothes, well-fitted clothes too, wore them with the ease and grace that few cattlemen or even townsmen ever acquired. Then the man started to cross the street. As he came up on the walk, some of the men who had just emerged from the lunchroom quickly moved out of his way. He gave Canavan a nod.

"I owe you an apology, Canavan," he said, his lips parting in a smile. Smooth-shaven, with a touch of gray at his temples, he had small, almost delicate features, and small, white, even teeth. "I had no idea you were so handy with your gun."

"I know which end of it to hold," Canavan answered.

The man laughed.

"Yes, I think you do," he said. "Mike Hoban said he thought you'd be quite good and I should have accepted his opinion and acted accordingly. But Mike unfortunately has a tendency to exaggerate at times, and I was afraid this might be one of them. But had I known how expert you are, I'd have selected some real gun-hands for the job. Then we'd have had a real show."

"You can send them after me the next time, Harp," Canavan said evenly.

"I don't think there would be any need for a next time if we could sit down and talk a bit."

"And what would we talk about?"

"I wonder if you wouldn't find my office more comfortable and certainly a lot more private than the street?"

"That depends on what you want to talk about, doesn't it?"

"We-ll, suppose it was of a personal nature?"

"You don't know me, Harp, and I don't know you. So how personal could we get?"

"Suppose I wanted to tell you of the plans I've made and how you could be fitted into them? To your advantage, of course."

"Don't think I'd be interested in hearing them, Harp. I don't want anybody making plans for me or that include me. I want to make them myself and for myself, and I want to carry them out myself. Y'see, I'm a loner. Working alone, I don't have to worry about pleasing anybody 'cept myself. That way, I go where I like and when I like and I do what I like. I stay as long or as short as I like and I like it that way. And I aim to keep doing things that way."

"I'm sure you've heard it said that in unity there is strength."

"Yeah, sure."

"Then you won't dispute me when I say that an organization always stands a far better chance of succeeding in whatever it sets out to do than an individual. And an organization is what I am building."

"For what purpose, Harp? For instance, like going after and wiping out poor, defenceless people like homesteaders, and it doesn't matter a damn to you if there are women and children included among them? No, Harp, that's not for me. I don't want any part of that kind of deal. What's more, because that's the kind of deal you go for, I don't want any part of you, your plans or your organization."

Hitching up his levis, Canavan stepped around Harp and started to walk away from him: he stopped, looked back at him and said: "The plans you oughta be making oughta be for the hereafter, for how you're gonna make your peace where you're going with everybody there knowing even before you get there what a low, murdering skunk you are."

IV

The startling thunder of gunfire had brought Christopher Daws rushing out to the street. Skidding to a stop on the walk in front of his office, he looked downstreet wonderingly. He saw men spill out of doorways and alleys and converge upon a spot directly opposite the lunchroom.

"The direction they're looking in, whatever it was that happened must have taken place in the lunchroom," he decided. "Probably a couple of Harp's killers had a falling out and settled it in their usual way."

He was about to turn and go back inside when some of the onlookers started to cross the street. He followed them with his eyes. He stared a little in surprise when he recognized the tall figure standing in front of the lunchroom. He saw men pass Canavan and gather around the doorway and poke their heads inside, saw them back off again and make way for a man who emerged holding his right wrist rather tightly with his left hand, and who plodded off in the direction of the saloon. But then a lone figure crossing the street to the lunchroom caught his eye.

"Harp," he muttered and his mouth tightened. He frowned when he saw Harp step up on the walk and say something to Canavan. The latter answered. The conversation between the two men was brief. However Daws couldn't help but wish he was there so that he could hear it. When he saw Canavan step around Harp, say a final word to him, and without waiting for Harp to answer, start up the street, Daws felt better for it. A steely light burned in his eyes. "Whatever it was that Canavan just told him, I don't think Harp liked it. Judging by the way he looked after Canavan, I don't think he liked it one little bit."

The evening shadows, Canavan noticed as he strode upstreet, had already begun to drape themselves over the town. He could see them lengthening and deepening, and he knew that the transition from evening to night would be swift. Spotting Daws who was still standing in front of his boarded-up office, Canavan quickened his pace. Daws saw him coming and backed inside. When Canavan came abreast of the place, slowed his step and peered in, Daws beckoned to him, and Canavan cut across the walk and entered.

"How'd you make out?" he asked.

"Not as good as I had hoped," was Daws' reply. "So far, only two out of seven."

"When do you think they'll be able to pull out?"

"In a couple of days. Becker, the tailor, thinks he should be able to slip away possibly sometime Friday night. The Standards, the people who own that little yard-goods place up the street, would like to see if they can't collect some of the money people in town owe them before they clear out. Figure them for Saturday or Sunday at the latest."

Canavan nodded and commented: "You've made a start, and that's important. 'Course I don't know how much those two storekeepers have been handing over to Harp every week. The point is though –"

"Between Becker and the Standards, about fifteen dollars a week," Daws interrupted. "They're small fry, you know. Their places of business are just, we-ll, holes in the walls."

"That's all right. Fifteen bucks is still fifteen bucks," Canavan maintained, "and it will make a difference to Harp next week when he gets around to adding up and finds his take that much less than he's been getting up to now."

"Y-es," Daws conceded. "I suppose he will notice it and wonder."

" 'Course he will," Canavan assured him. "Now if you can talk a couple more into closing up, that'll make the difference even bigger and even more noticeable to Harp. How many are there left to talk to?"

"The same number I talked to today. Seven more. However, these seven are the bigger ones."

"That's nice. Think you can go after them the first thing tomorrow morning?"

"I plan to see one and possibly two of them tonight."

"Good for you."

"Might find it to be an even better time to talk to them than during the day when they're waiting on trade and listening to me only in between times."

"That's right," Canavan agreed.

"What's been happening to you meantime?"

"Oh, nothing much."

Daws smiled.

"What was all that excitement about down the street?" he asked.

"A couple of Harp's gun-throwers tried to brace me when I was having something to eat in the lunchroom."

"You don't look any the worse for it, so apparently they weren't overly successful."

"No. I've been braced before, and by a lot better than they were," Canavan answered gravely. "Harp had a third man posted outside, but he was too scared to death to do anything. Ran off when I came out."

"Probably thought better of it."

"Yeah, guess he did. He pegged a shot at me just before he started to make a run for it."

"Harp will think twice before he sends him out again after you."

"I could have got him too. But I felt sorry for him and I let him get away."

"By the way, Canavan, wasn't that Harp I saw talking to you after the shooting?"

"Yeah. Wanted me to sit down in his office and have a little talk with him."

"You don't say! That's more than he ever asked me to do."

Canavan grinned.

"You don't wear a gun," he answered. "Maybe that makes a difference to him."

"Meaning that while he obviously fears the printed word, he doesn't fear it as much as he does a gun in the hands of a man who knows how to use it. And that being so, he doesn't have to try to make a deal with me. Yes, I can see where you and your gun might cause him concern, enough to warrant his making overtures to you."

"I told him I wasn't interested in what he might have to say," Canavan added, "and walked away from him."

"And now what?"

Canavan's broad shoulders lifted.

"I don't know," he replied. " 'Cept that from now on, I expect Harp to take a whack at me every chance he gets."

"I'm afraid so, Canavan. You'll be facing stiff odds," Daws warned. "He has a good-sized crew at his command."

"Then I'll have to shoot faster and straighter than his hands do. So long, Daws."

Daws didn't answer. He moved to the doorway after Canavan, watched him stride on up the street, saw him cross over and go into the hotel. Then he backed inside again and closed the door.

The hotel-keeper was behind the counter when Canavan entered the lobby. He looked up, nodded, and when Canavan came up to the counter, he said: "Evening. Got somebody waiting for you, Mister."

"That so?"

The man nodded again, and smiled a little.

"A lady," he added. "And a right pretty one too. She's waiting for you upstairs. Figured she might as well sit while she was waiting, so I showed her where your room is and let her in."

It was, as Canavan expected it would be, Mrs. Lundy. She had carried the room's only chair, a stiff, straight-backed and uninviting-looking affair, over to the window, and was sitting there, looking down into the darkening street. She twisted around instantly when the door opened and Canavan entered the room.

"Oh," she said, and she flushed a little, and got up on her feet. Black-clad, she smoothed down the front of her dress. There was no question about it; she was pretty, and the touch of color in her cheeks made her look even prettier. "The man downstairs said I could wait in here for you. I hope you don't mind."

"No," he told her, thumbing his hat up from his forehead. "I don't mind." He sauntered forward, stopped again when he came to the bed. "I have to admit though I didn't think you'd ever have the nerve to want to see me again."

Her flush deepened.

"Didn't take you very long," he taunted, "to spill what you knew to Harp, did it?"

"You haven't any right to say that!" she protested. "You don't know what happened."

"I know enough, all I have to know. I told you what it would mean to me if Harp found out that I was the one who helped your husband break out of the sheriff's office. That my life wouldn't be worth a plugged dime. Didn't I? Just to prove to you that I knew what I was talking about, Harp's men tried to brace me this evening. Tried to kill me."

She caught her breath, put her hand over her mouth to stifle the gasp that came surging upward within her.

"And I can thank you for that."

"You don't understand!" she cried. "I didn't mean to tell them. Honestly, I didn't!"

"The point is, you did tell them though, didn't you?"

"Yes!"

"Well?"

"You don't know what happened. They frightened me so, I didn't know what I was doing or . . . or saying."

She was crying. Tears had filled her eyes and were trickling down her cheeks. She dabbed at them with a small, balled-up handkerchief, and wiped her cheeks, streaking them.

"I'm sorry about that, about them frightening you. But that's it, Mrs. Lundy. The end. I was willing to go along with you for a time, help you till you got yourself settled in town and you found something to do, to work at, so you'd be able to take care of yourself. But that was as far as I was willing to go, and I told you that. We-ell, I'll stretch it a point. I'll give you another couple of dollars. But that's all." He dug inside his pants, squeezed a couple of rolled-up bills out of his money belt, counted out five dollars and tossed them on the bed, and put the rest in his pocket. "There's five dollars. Take it."

She lifted her tear-filled eyes from the money to him.

"I've used the money you gave me for my room and board for the week," she told him, "and now I owe three dollars for this dress. I had to have a black dress for Ben's funeral, you know."

"Yeah, I guess you did. But I'm not married to you, you know. So don't expect me to pay for it. 'Fraid that's something you'll have to work out for yourself, along with everything else from now on."

"But I told the man I'd pay for the dress today. That I'd have the money for it today."

"All right. You've got some money. That five." He pointed to the bills on the bed. A couple of them had begun to curl up again at the ends. "Pay him out of that."

"I can't," she protested. "If I do, I'll only have two dollars left."

"Suit yourself," he said with a shrug. "It's none of my business what you do. But just to satisfy my curiosity, you mind telling me where you expected to get the money for the dress? Did you think you were gonna sucker me into that too?"

"You owe me that," she flung at him, flushing again, "and more too!"

"I don't owe you a thing," he said flatly, "and I'm getting doggoned fed-up hearing you say that. I think you'd better get out of here before I really tell you what I think of you."

He turned on his heel and went to the door,

opened it, and backing with it, opened it wide, held it steady and waited. She snatched up the money from the bed and flounced doorward with the bills clutched tightly in her fist. She stopped a step short of the doorway, glowered at him and said: "You're responsible for me, for what happens to me, and don't you think for even a minute that I'm going to let you shirk that responsibility."

" 'Bye, Mrs. Lundy," he said and moved with the door.

Hastily, to avoid the closing door, she crossed the threshold. He heard her step on the stairs as he stood backed against the door. When it faded out, he walked away from the door, shaking his head. Suddenly he realized that it was dark. He scratched a match head with his thumbnail, and when it burst into flame, burning against the shadows with yellow-and-red-tinged, flickering light, he crossed at once to the bureau and lit the lamp. He took off his hat and stood with it in his hand, running his finger around the inside of the sweatband. Then, annoyed with himself for having permitted the Lundy woman to make such a fool of him, he gave vent to his feelings by angrily scaling his hat away. It soared in circling flight and climbed to about three-quarters of the way up the side wall beyond the bed, struck and caromed off. But instead of dropping on the bed, it plummeted downward, in toward the wall, and fell between it and the bed. Scowling darkly, he pulled the bed away from the wall, and squeezing into the space between the two, bent to pick up his hat. A rifle cracked startlingly, and an ominously whining bullet struck the bedpost inches beyond his hand. Instinctively he flung himself downward and landed on the floor on top of his hat, crushing it under him. He cursed and, twisting around despite the limited space, managed to yank his gun out of his holster.

In an angry effort to reply to his attacker, he crawled under the bed and headed for the window; sensing though that he would be making a target of himself once he raised his head above the sill when he sought to locate the rifleman, he stopped and began to back off. Wriggling backward on his belly and propelling himself by his bent arms, he pushed himself again under the bed and crept the full length of it in the direction of the door. He stopped briefly to get his breath, and went on again till he came to the door.

He lay flat for a moment, panting and wheezing and heaving a little, then shifting his gun to his left hand and half twisting over on his side, reached up with his right hand, turned the knob and opened the door.

Flat again, he maneuvered himself over the threshold and out of the room, pulled the door shut from outside, and scrambled to his feet. A second rifle shot ploughed into the door, splintering one of the panels, and he spun away from it hastily.

At the far end of the dimly lighted landing he could see a wall ladder, and he ran to it and looked up. The way to the roof was open to him; he could see dark sky overhead. Gun in hand, he climbed the rungs and emerged in darkness. Hunching over as he stepped off the ladder, and getting down again on his hands and knees, he crawled across the roof toward the front of the building, stopped just short of the lipped edge and peered over. Directly across the street and a floor below him, on the flat roof of what appeared to be a vacant store, crouched a shadowy figure. Canavan's eyes hardened as he watched the man. When the latter raised up a bit and night light glinted for the barest instant on the barrel of his rifle, Canavan's gun leveled. The man stood up then and moved closer to the edge, apparently trying to get a better view of Canavan's room. The leveled Colt roared and the rifleman staggered, lurched drunkenly and pitched off the roof and crashed on the walk below.

There was no reaction in the street for

perhaps a minute or two. Then Canavan heard windows run up, heard doors open, and saw heads poked out. A couple of men appeared below him, stood together for a moment on the walk in front of the hotel; a third man carrying a lighted lantern joined them and led the way across the street to where the rifleman lay in a heap. The light from the lantern played over the fallen man, adding a somewhat eerie touch to the scene. Other men came up, too, and gathered around the motionless figure. A man who had knelt down and bent over him got up again; when the others looked at him and he shook his head, Canavan knew he had again lessened the odds against him. Holstering his gun, he backed away, turned around and retraced his steps to the ladder and made his way down the rungs.

As he stepped off the ladder onto the landing, someone standing at the head of the stairs looked at him, started toward him and called: "Wondered where you'd gone to, Mister. You all right?"

It was the hotel-keeper.

"Yeah, sure," Canavan answered. He came together with the man in front of his room and pointed to the splintered door. "Sorry about that, partner."

The bald-headed man glanced at it and

said: "Wasn't your fault, so forget it."

"Maybe I'd better clear out of here before they show up again and do an even better job of shooting up the place," Canavan suggested, and added: "No reason for you to take a walloping on account of me."

"And where do you think you'd find another place, Mister? This is the only hotel in town, you know."

"Oh, I'd hunt around and chances are come up with something."

The man smiled and said: "Suppose we talk about that some other time, huh? Kinda think some sleep might do the two of us some good being that it's getting late now. You don't think they'll make another try tonight, do you?"

"No-o, I don't think so. But there's no telling, you know."

"Then just in case they do show up again tonight, suppose we bed you down in another room and make it tougher for them to find you?"

"Whatever you say," Canavan responded.

"Got a small room downstairs, kinda hidden away so that anybody looking for it would have a time finding it. Ought to be just the place for you."

When the man turned and started down the stairs, Canavan trooped after him.

In the morning when he appeared in the lobby, the front door opened and the hotel man came in from the street with a broom in his hand.

"Morning," he said. He propped up the broom in a corner. "Sleep all right?"

"Slept fine," Canavan told him, grinned and added: "Like I didn't have a care in the world."

"Figuring on going out now?"

"Sure. You don't think I'm going to let them get the idea they've scared me into holing up, do you?"

"No, 'course not," was the quick answer. "I asked because this is the time if you wanna go out. I had a pretty good look around while I was sweeping up outside and there wasn't any sign that I could see of any of Harp's hellions. Too early for them to be up and doing, I guess." Canavan made no reply and the man went on with: "They must know by now you'll give them as good as you get, so I don't look for them to try anything in broad daylight. When they come after you again, I expect they'll do it at night, figuring it'll be safer for them then."

He moved aside then and Canavan, shifting his holster a little and bringing the butt of his gun more directly below his right hand, stepped outside and stood for a minute with his hands raised, curling the brim of his hat. The hotel-keeper, standing behind him in the doorway, said: "That feller you shot off the roof last night, there was no sign of him when I came out this morning. They must've lugged him away before that. The walk's wet though. Notice it? Somebody must've flushed the blood off it with a bucket of water."

Canavan nodded and strode off down the street. Storekeepers, the earliest risers, sweeping off the walk in front of their establishments, lifted their gaze when he came along; they met his eyes and promptly looked away again and went on plying their brooms. The *Clarion*'s door was open and Canavan walked into the office.

"Be right with you," a voice that he recognized at once as Daws' informed him. He seated himself in the chair at Daws' desk, but just as he squared back in it, the stocky editor appeared, nodded a greeting, and said: "That shooting I heard last night . . ."

"That was our friend Harp taking another crack at me."

"That's what I thought. It didn't last very long though, did it? Two or three shots and that was it."

"Needed only one shot to end it."

"I see."

"Sa-ay, Daws, the feller who runs the hotel —"

"His name is Voss. Sam Voss. But what about him?"

"What's he got it in for Harp any more than anyone else has?" Canavan asked.

"The first day Harp took over the saloon, Sam's brother Willie stopped in for a glass of beer. He had a run-in with one of Harp's killers. Willie never had a chance. He was bullet-riddled before he could get his own gun out."

"So that's it! Just wondered. Thanks for telling me. Oh, how'd you do last night?"

"Better than I did during the day. Hoskins who owns the general store up the street pulled out last night after midnight."

"Oh, swell!"

"That isn't all. Carl Drews' swap shop next door to Hoskins' place is closed too. He followed Hoskins out of Paradise."

"Wait till Harp gets wind of that!"

"Hoskins was paying Harp twenty-five dollars a week. Drews only five. Together though, thirty dollars a week, and if that doesn't make Harp do a little extra thinking..."

"Add that thirty to the fifteen those other two have been handing over —"

"Oh, you mean Becker and the Standards?"

"Yeah. Comes to forty-five bucks a week or a hundred an' eighty a month. And believe me, that's something."

"Gillis, the old fool who runs the Emporium, is finding it hard to get up the twenty dollars he has to pay Harp every week. Still he's afraid to do anything to help himself. Harp's thrown such a scare into some people, they're even afraid to whisper his name. That's Gillis. Full of complaints but unwilling to do anything about them. Oh, by the way, Canavan, Ardis Lundy –"

"Ardis, huh? Picked a fancy name for herself, didn't she?"

"It probably was her mother who did the picking, wouldn't you say?"

"I suppose," Canavan answered a little grumpily.

"Don't tell me you've had another session with the lady?"

"And how I did!" Canavan said disgustedly and he heaved himself up from Daws' chair. He repeated the story of Mrs. Lundy's call upon him the previous evening. "You know, Daws, you can argue with a man and when he won't let himself see things the way you're explaining them to him, you can pick up something and bust him over the head with it, and have every reason to believe you've beat some sense into his thick skull. But with a woman..."

He didn't finish; he stopped and shook his head sadly.

"I know," Daws said. "But while you were telling me that story, Canavan, something came to me, and I've been mulling it over and wondering if it isn't in line with the curious workings of a woman's mind. In this case of course, Ardis Lundy's."

"I'm listening."

"Canavan, I wonder if Ardis hasn't decided upon you to replace Ben."

Canavan's head jerked back. He looked hard at the smaller man.

Canavan snorted.

"You're crazier'n all get-out, Daws," he retorted. "I've heard some out-an'-out loco ideas in my time, but I know damned well I've never heard anything to top this one."

"Don't be so sure it's that crazy," Daws cautioned him. "It makes sense to me, although I will admit it does in a sort of, we-ell, crazy sort of a way."

Canavan stepped back from him and circling, began to edge toward the door.

"Just in case this craziness might be catching," he said, "I'm getting out of here and I'm gonna stay out of here."

Daws followed him to the door and said:

"The stores' closing will mean a shortage of foodstuffs here, Canavan. There will be no one to sell any, hence no one will be able to buy any. However, we'll eat, and we'll eat well too. I've prepared myself for such a situation. I had Hoskins bring over such a supply of his stock, from flour and sugar to bacon and coffee, that we two won't have to worry 'bout where our next meal is coming from for a long, long time."

"In that case," Canavan said wryly, settling his hat more firmly on his head, "I'll be back. That is, once the lunchroom closes or runs out of stuff."

Marching downstreet again toward the lunchroom, Canavan raised his eyes as he neared a two-story house with a sagging veranda fronting it and a sign jutting out over the walk and the legend on it reading: ROOMS FOR LADIES AND GENTLEMEN – *With or Without Meals*. He wondered if that was where Ardis Lundy – and he frowned when he thought of her – was living.

Just as he came within a stride or two of the house itself with the steps leading to the veranda twice that distance away, a rifle cracked and a bullet tore his hat from his head. He spun around after it instinctively, and lunged for it, missed and saw it flutter past his outflung hand. He took a step toward it and bent to pick it up; his booted foot touched it first and sent it skidding away. He made no further attempt to recover it. There was more demanding business at hand. He jerked out his gun, and, half turning around to look across the street, seeking the man who had fired at him, he scampered up to the house, and leveling his gun for a quick shot if the opportunity presented itself, backed up the steps to the veranda. A bullet that was fired at him from an alley diagonally across the street sang past him and buried itself high up in the woodwork above the door. He recognized the more authoritative voice of a Colt when another bullet splintered the veranda floor a step beyond him and, slanting downward, coursed deep into the wood. Backing again across the veranda to the door, he reached behind him, found the knob and turned it, and when the door opened, he quickly stepped inside and closed it. The upper panel of the door was made of glass and was covered by a half-curtain. A bullet shattered the glass and made the curtain fill and balloon backward; it slipped forward again and spewed bits and pieces of glass over the veranda and then hung a little limply over the empty panel.

Fire from both guns drummed again and riddled the door, and Canavan beat a hasty retreat. There was a narrow, carpeted flight of stairs beyond him, and just as he was about to bound up the steps, he heard quick footsteps close by and he stopped with his gun half-raised. A woman emerged from a nearby portiered doorway, stopped abruptly when she saw Canavan.

"Who . . . who are you?" she faltered. "And what are you doing in my house?"

She was short and pudgy and double-chinned. Because she had experienced something of a shock, encountering a strange man in her house with a gun in his hand, her momentary unnerving made her chins quiver. She wore a huge cameo at her throat, pinned to the high-necked bodice of her dress; when she gulped and swallowed and made a wry face, the cameo jerked.

"You'll have to leave at once," she said, drawing herself up to her full height. "If you don't," she shook a fat, stubby finger at Canavan, "I'll call the sheriff."

"I didn't mean to break in on you like this, lady," Canavan told her. "But I didn't have any choice. Now if you'll show me the way to the back door I'll . . ."

There was a heavy-handed pounding, and a

door was shaken and rattled somewhere at the rear of the house.

"Too late for that now," Canavan said. The woman's full, round face had begun to pale. "Looks like somebody else had the same idea only he beat me to it. Lady, if you've got a cellar, you'd better make tracks for it and stay put down there till this is over."

He stepped back from her, spun around and bounded up the stairs. Then topping the stairs and rounding the stairpost in full flight he collided heavily with someone who stepped out of a room and into his path. Together they fell and sprawled on the landing. Scrambling to his feet, Canavan bent to help the woman up. Angrily she pushed off his hands, got up by herself.

"Oh," she said, and her lip curled. He stared a little. It was Ardis Lundy. "So it's you, is it? And it's a good thing it is. I was going over to the hotel to see you. Now I won't have to. I paid the man for my dress, so you know how much I've got left. Mrs. Haber was up here a while ago and told me she wants my next week's board paid in advance, or I'll have to leave. Now that you're here, you can see her and pay her. You'll find her downstairs."

She flounced back to her room and slammed the door behind her.

V

Canavan liked to think of himself as a rather well-poised, self-possessed and deliberate individual, and one who had been specially endowed with the ability to meet and cope with any situation that might arise. However he was anything but poised and deliberate at that moment. Actually he was furious, not only with Ardis Lundy, whose calm audacity had left him almost speechless, but with himself for having permitted her to make him a party to her ridiculous way of thinking. Muttering darkly, he cursed the luck that had brought him to Paradise in the first place. Then because he had to vent his feelings upon someone other than himself, he damned Ben Lundy for having been so downright pig-headed as to have brought about his own untimely death, thus involving Canavan with the homesteader's astonishingly unreasonable widow. Scowling, he retraced his steps to the head of the stairs and peered below. He stood, head bent, listening for some sound that would betray the presence of the back-door intruder whom Canavan was certain had managed to force his way into the house, probably while the Lundy woman and he were busy disentangling themselves. But he couldn't hear anything despite his straining efforts, and after a minute he stepped back. When he noticed some thin rays of sunlight playing over a small stretch of landing floor, he ranged his gaze upward and found they were coming in through a small, square window at the front end of the upper floor. He hurried to it, and, standing on tiptoe because the window was unusually high up, he stole a look into the street.

He saw three men come dashing up and turn in to an alley opposite the boarding house. Harp, he told himself grimly, had finally made a concentrated effort to dispose of him. The man at the back door, the two who had fired at him earlier, and now three more men, made six. Assigning so many of his crew to the attack on Canavan was ample proof of how seriously Harp viewed Canavan's threat to his grip on Paradise. It was possible, too, that even more of Harp's outfit were taking a hand in the fray than he suspected. Others might have piled into the alley unseen by him when his attention was focused elsewhere. That made him think of Ardis Lundy, and thinking of her made him scowl again too.

He froze suddenly, when he thought he

had heard something. He turned slowly, settled himself again on the full flats of his feet, bent a little and tiptoed back to the stairway, crouched down and peered between the banister uprights. A shadow fell across the lower floor. Then he saw the bent-over figure of a man. He drew back a little and waited to see what the man would do. He hadn't long to wait, perhaps no more than a moment or two. Creeping up to the stairway, the man looked up, planted one foot on the first step and stood motionless, apparently listening. Then, raising his gun, he started to climb. The stairs creaked thinly under him as he negotiated them. He stopped when he reached the halfway mark, turned his head and looked down. Then, squaring around again and lifting his eyes, he continued to climb. When he was some three or four steps from the top, Canavan arose and, holding his gun on him, glided noiselessly around the stairpost to the head of the stairs, backed a little and stood there. The oncoming man stopped instantly, stiff-frozen in his tracks, when he saw the towering figure above him, blocking his way. He did not move for a moment, then he stole a quick look below him, apparently measuring the distance to the lower floor and estimating his chances of escaping if he decided to . . .

"Yeah?" Canavan asked tauntingly,

interrupting the man's conjecturing.

The latter looked up again. But he made no answer. He appeared to be looking at Canavan; however he wasn't. Instead his eyes were fixed on Canavan's leveled gun, more particularly on its fire-blackened muzzle which must have gaped at him with a seemingly widening, yawning mouth the longer he stared at it.

"Well?" Canavan demanded impatiently. "What's it gonna be? What are you gonna do?"

There was no retreating then, and Harp's man must have realized it, just as he must have known that he had no alternative. His decision made for him, his gun flashed upward. But it was too late. Before he could fire, Canavan's leveled gun thundered deafeningly. At point-blank range there was no missing his target. The man gasped as the lead slugs slammed into his body and drove the breath out of him. He tottered brokenly and dropped his gun. It fell at his feet, slid off the step on which he was standing and toppled to the step below. He sagged and lay against the wall for a moment, his chest heaving. He lifted his eyes to Canavan, and the latter, holding his fire now, saw death in them. The man fell backward and struck heavily; his body arched and flipped over, and he tumbled down the stairs and landed in a sprawled-out heap against the first step. Ardis Lundy's door opened and she peered out. When she spied Canavan, she opened the door wider and stepped outside.

"What . . . what's happened?" she asked.

He didn't answer, just lifted his eyes and glanced at her and looked away again. She came sweeping down the landing to the stairway, peered over the banister rail and promptly gasped.

"Don't tell me you've done it again?"

He looked hard at her.

"Don't tell me you've interfered again in someone else's business and that that," she pointed to the hunched-over body lying at the foot of the stairs, "that's the result of it?"

"Go back to your room," he told her curtly, "and stay put there. Better get down under your bed while you're at it." Gunfire suddenly thundered, and the street door shook under the blasting. "Those are real bullets they're shooting, and they aren't at all fussy 'bout who they hit. Go on now. Get back inside."

He didn't wait for her to answer; he went down the stairs, stepped over the body of Harp's man and, crouching down against the wall, began to inch his way forward to the riddled door. He dove floorward instantly when another volley bracketed the door. The sagging, glass-filled half-curtain was shot off and it fell with a tinkling sound. Tiny bits and long, jagged-edged slivers spilled out over the floor. Stealing a guarded look outside, Canavan saw a man come skidding across the street, saw him leap up on the walk and start up the steps to the veranda. Canavan's gun voiced a protest. His bullet caught the man just as he stepped up on the veranda, hurled him backward and dumped him on the walk. He tried to get up shortly, but the effort was too much for him. He lay on his belly for a couple of minutes, then he maneuvered himself around so that he lay facing the house. Slowly he forced himself up, propped himself up on his elbows, leveled his gun and fired twice through the shattered door. With another effort that must have exacted a heavy toll of his fast-ebbing strength, he managed to get himself up on his knees. He leveled his gun for still another shot when Canavan's second bullet hit him. He stiffened, dropped his gun and pitched out over the walk on his face.

There was a momentary hush. Then gunfire broke out again, a brisk, steady fire that raked the front of the house from the veranda up to the very top of it. But there were no more attempts to storm the house.

Backing away from where he had been crouching to the side of the door, Canavan stopped long enough to reload his gun, then he went on, whipped through the portiered doorway and into the kitchen. The back door stood ajar, actually flung back, and its shattered lock hung from it, proof of the manner in which the first man had managed to gain an entrance into the house. Cautiously, Canavan stole a look outside. When he was reasonably satisfied that there was no one lurking about in the back yard, he slipped out and, hugging the back walls of the buildings, made his way to Daws' place. The stocky man came at once in response to Canavan's hurried knocking on the *Clarion*'s back door, and admitted him.

"Had yourself a time of it again with Harp's gun-throwers, didn't you?" he asked, bolting the door. "How many of them did you get this time?"

"Two," Canavan told him. "Sorry Harp wasn't one of them."

"Not much chance of that, I'm afraid, while he still has others to do his bidding. But if you last long enough, and your luck stays with you, you're liable to whittle down the odds against you to a very favorable number that eventually might include him." Daws followed Canavan into the office proper. "You were wearing a hat when you left here, weren't you? Lost it in your travels?"

"That's when it started," Canavan explained. "When some polecat pot-shot me from across the street and put a slug in my hat."

"Better there than in your head," the editor said dryly. "By the way, I happened to look up the street right after you left here and I saw some of Harp's men trying the doors of a couple of the stores that have closed. The not-too-amiable gentlemen appeared to be a little surprised at first, then they looked genuinely concerned. I wonder what Paradise's good friend, the judge, had to say when they reported the matter to him?"

"Shouldn't take too much imagination to figure that one out. I didn't get to the lunchroom, you know, so I still haven't had any breakfast."

"I think we can do something about that for you," Daws said. He pointed to a small, closed door in a far, dark corner. "That door leads to the kitchen."

"Mean I have to go fix things for myself? That the kind of host you are?"

"I supply the fixings, my friend. From then on, it's up to you."

Canavan gave him a hard look that did not disturb him in the least and, grumbling a little to himself, trudged off in the direction that Daws had indicated.

An hour later, again making his way through the back yards, he returned to the hotel and entered it just as Sam Voss was emerging from behind his counter. Voss stopped at once.

"Say, that woman's back," he announced to Canavan. "The same one who came looking for you last night."

Canavan frowned.

"Said she wanted a room near yours," Voss continued. "So I put her next door to you, in Number Four. Said she didn't know for how long she'd want the room, and told me to take it up with you, being that you'd be paying her bill."

Canavan's frown darkened into a scowl.

"I got an even better look at her this time," the hotel-keeper went on. "Better than I did last night. Not that I don't still think she's the same good-looker that I thought she was. She sure is, Mister. Only this time there was something kinda familiar about her. Seems to me I've seen her before. Mister, wasn't she married to that nester feller they were fixin' to hang the other morning? That Lundy who broke out of the sheriff's office and got himself shot to pieces before he could get away?"

"She upstairs now?"

"Yeah, sure."

Grim-faced and a little flushed, Canavan climbed the stairs, strode past his own room and the splintered door to it, and, halting squarely in front of Number Four, knocked on it heavy-handedly. There was no answer, no sound of movement in the room.

"Try it again, Mister," Voss called from below, and Canavan, turning his head, saw him standing at the foot of the stairs and looking up at him. "Might be the lady's takin' a nap, you know."

Canavan didn't answer. He squared around again and raised his hand to knock a second time; he stayed his hand, lowered it, when he heard a quick footstep behind the closed door, and then a voice that he recognized.

"Ye-es?"

"Canavan," he said curtly. "Open up. Want to talk to you."

"Oh, just a minute, please!"

He looked downstairs again as he stepped back from the door. Voss flushed a little under Canavan's hard eyes and walked away. There was a moment-long wait, then he heard a key turn and grate in the lock, and the door was opened. He glowered at Ardis Lundy who was framed in the doorway.

"Now don't blame me for this," she said

quickly, before he could speak. "Mrs. Haber put me out and you can thank yourself for that."

"I can, huh?" he retorted. "Suppose you tell me what I had to do with it?"

A faint flush was riding in her cheeks; now it began to spread and deepen.

"Well," she began, "when the shooting was over and I looked for you and couldn't find you, and I couldn't help but wonder, that is, whether you had managed to slip out of the house and had made your way to some safe place, or if those men who were after you had finally broken in, overpowered you and taken you away, or if –"

" 'Course," he interrupted. "I can understand how awfully worried you must've been. It isn't every day you manage to hook on to a prize sucker, and when you do land one, you wouldn't want anything to happen to him."

She made no response, no comment; in fact, she gave no indication that she had even heard him. She moistened her lips with the tip of her tongue, and went on with her recital with annoying calm.

"Mrs. Haber, who was with me, thought it odd that I should show any interest in you, supposedly a stranger to me as well as to her, in view of the fact that I had told her that I knew no one in Paradise. So I had to offer some kind of explanation. I suppose that what I told her, confessing that I hadn't told her everything, and that I did have one friend, you, must have sounded rather lame and made her pretty little mind jump to nasty conclusions, judging by the way she looked at me. And the way she kept saying, 'H'm,' I wanted to shake her because I could tell what she was thinking. She insisted that you wouldn't have come there if I hadn't been there, and the trouble wouldn't have happened. She said someone – and I knew she meant you or me by that – had to pay for the damage done to her house. Since you had gone, and I couldn't very well pay her and told her so, she made me get my things together and leave."

"H'm," he said.

"Please," she said. "That's Mrs. Haber's very own expression and it seems to fit her. If you can't make any other comment, don't say anything. Now where was I? Oh, yes . . . since I didn't have enough money to go to another boarding house –"

He interrupted again with: "You came here because you knew I was here."

"Yes," she said simply.

"That's what I figured. Got some news for you, Mrs. Lundy. I'm through with you, finished, washed up. I don't intend to give you another buck. As for you staying here, that isn't up to me. That's up to Voss, the feller who runs this place. I don't care a damn what you do, or where you do it, and I don't aim to be suckered into anything else for you. I'm gonna tell that to Voss too, although chances are he's listening to this right now so maybe I won't have to repeat this to him later on. Anyway, long as he knows I don't aim to make good on anything for you, what he does about you is up to him. I don't want to know anything about it."

He wheeled away from her, walked to his own door, opened it, went inside and slammed the door behind him. He retraced his steps to it and locked it. Then he went to the window and drew down the blind about two-thirds of the way, moved the chair away from in front of the window to an off-to-a-side position and seated himself. He checked his gun, made sure that it was fully loaded, and sat back, grim-faced, and with his arms folded over his chest. He tried hard to put Ardis Lundy out of his thoughts; when she refused to be shunted aside, he gave up, shook his head sadly. He sat motionlessly, hunched over, and staring down into the street. He heard bootsteps on the stairs, but he did not look up. When he heard a knock, he frowned and half turned doorward, finally got up on his feet and trudged to the door.

"Yeah?" he asked grumpily.

"Voss," was the reply. "Got a note for you."

He unlocked the door, opened it; the hotelkeeper handed him a small, folded square of paper, and said low-voiced: "That newspaper feller asked me to see that you got it."

"Oh," Canavan answered. "Thanks."

"Yeah, sure."

Canavan carried it back with him to his chair, and sinking down in it, unfolded the note. It was pencil-scribbled and read:

Closing tonight; Gillis, Murtaugh and Mailler. Twenty, fifteen and five dollars weekly respectively. Brings the number to seven, and the weekly loss to our mutual friend, to eighty-five dollars. Owe Gillis an apology. Didn't think he had the courage. Proves one must never pass too hasty judgment on fellowman. Will now go after the others with renewed vigor.

D.

Canavan crumpled the piece of paper into a ball and stuffed it in his pocket. Harp, he was sure, was furious when he was told about the previous night's closing; when the new closings were reported to him the next morning, he would be doubly furious. But once his fury had passed, and if he was as smart as Canavan thought him, he would read the signs, the handwriting on the wall, and do something. But would he decide that he had worn out his welcome in Paradise, and abandon it, and go elsewhere? That was the question, and Canavan, a realist, wasn't at all willing to believe that that would be Harp's decision. In fact, that would be the man's last decision. He would try in every way, Canavan was confident, to stand his ground and retreat only when there was no alternative.

Even then, it wouldn't be his blood that would be spilled or his life that would pay for his defense; the men whom he had gathered around him and those who had taken refuge under his banner would be the ones upon whom that privilege would fall. That was the way it would be, the way it had always been for those who led and for those who followed. When the leader's bid for power was challenged, his followers did as they were expected to do; they stood firm and fought his fight for him while he urged them on from a safe place at the rear. But when he saw the tide of battle turning against him, it was he who broke and fled, leaving them to stand and fight on and die. Eventually he would turn up again, as loud-voiced and defiant as ever, and this time with a horde of new followers to fight his fight for him. The same old story would be repeated, and it would continue to be repeated as long as there were men to lead and others to follow.

Canavan slid down a little in his chair with his long legs thrust out in front of him. He squirmed and slumped down on the tail of his spine. After a bit, his eyes closed and he dozed off.

He awoke with a start, jerked upright in his chair when he felt someone nudge him and, twisting back and away, threw up his own hand to shield his eyes from the rays of a lighted lamp that was being held close by. Through his flexed fingers he saw that it was a woman who was holding the lamp, and that the woman was Ardis Lundy. He frowned and asked grumpily: "Oh, it's you again, huh? How'd you get in here?"

"Luckily for you, the door was unlocked. Hurry now. They're coming after you again."

"Huh?" He stared at her. His senses were still a little sleep-dulled. He blinked and made a wry face, and asked dully: "Who . . . who's coming after me?"

"Oh, for goodness sake," she said with a show of impatience. "You aren't awake yet.

Those men who were after you this morning."

"Oh," he said, and he sounded and looked fully awake then.

"They're coming up the street."

He got to his feet at once and drew his gun.

"Come on," she said over her shoulder as she turned with the lamp in her hand and walked doorward. "We haven't any too much time as it is."

"Wait a minute," he commanded. "Where are we going?"

"To my room."

"What's the idea?"

"You'll see."

"No," he answered with a shake of his head. "You keep out of this. Gunplay's nothing for a woman to get mixed up in. You get out of here and go find yourself a place where you'll be safe."

She opened the door and stood astride the threshold, lighting up the doorway and the landing immediately outside his room.

"You haven't a chance against so many of them," she told him evenly. "There must be at least a dozen of them according to Mr. Voss."

"Yeah? And I suppose you've got a better way to beat them off than with this, huh?" He pointed to his half-raised gun.

"Yes, I think so. At least, you'll stand a far

better chance doing what I have in mind than you will with your gun." He didn't move. "Well?" she demanded. "Going to stand there and wait for them to break in here and shoot you down like a dog the way they did Ben?"

He hesitated, debating with himself for perhaps a moment, then with a lift to his shoulders, he came striding across the room and trooped out after her.

"The door," she said. "I think you'd better close it."

He grunted, stopped and backed a couple of steps and reached for the doorknob, grasped it with his curled hand and yanked the door shut. She had walked on and was waiting for him in the doorway of her room. She turned as he came up to her and he followed her inside. She placed the lamp on the bureau opposite the bed and whipped back the bedcovers.

"All right, get in," she said, stepping back. When he hesitated again, she said impatiently: "It's your only chance. And nothing's going to happen to you, I assure you. In bed, I mean."

He holstered his gun.

"Take the side nearest the wall," she directed and began to unbutton her dress. "I'll get in on this side. Pull up the covers around you so they won't be able to see that you aren't undressed."

She removed her dress and draped it over

a nearby chair and turned to face him clad in a white camisole that was drawn together tightly over her firm, young breasts by a thin blue ribbon that wound in and out through a row of eyelets at the top of the garment and was bow-tied in the middle. Below was a long, full, black petticoat. She flushed under his wide eyes.

"You don't have to stare at me," she said severely. "Get into bed."

He stepped past her, climbed into bed and moved toward the wall. The light in the lamp went out and she got in beside him. She lay flat on her back for a moment or so, only about half-covered he judged since he hadn't felt her draw them up, then she sat up, apparently listening, suddenly turned to him and whispered: "They're here."

"Yeah," he breathed back at her. "I hear them. They're talking to Voss. Leastways I think it was him answering them."

"Covered up?"

"All the way to my chin."

"Good. Now listen to me. They'll be coming upstairs any minute now. They'll try your door first. When they find you aren't in your room, they'll probably search all the others, this one right after yours. When they open the door, don't move. Don't do anything. Pretend you're asleep.

Understand? I'll be the indignant one and I'll do the talking. The screaming too if I think it's necessary."

"Right."

"I think you'd better move just a little closer and turn to me," she went on in a hushed voice, and quickly added: "Now just because I want this to look natural, don't let it give you any ideas."

"This wasn't my idea in the first place, remember?"

"I know, but just the same, don't –"

She stopped abruptly, hastily slid down and drew up the covers. He brought himself closer to her, turned on his side to her too, as she had instructed. There were heavy bootsteps on the stairs and presently on the landing also. They heard hoarse whispering outside, heard the door to Canavan's room fling open, heard it thump as it flew back and struck the wall.

"All right, Canavan," a gruff voice that was phlegmy too, commanded. "Come outta there."

"Yeah," another voice added: "And throw out your gun first."

There was a brief silence, then a shuffling of feet, and: "Come outta there, you son-uva-bitch, or we'll blast you out!"

"Fellers," another voice that sounded like Voss' said from a little farther off than the others, probably from the foot of the stairs. "You're wasting your time. He isn't here. Went out about an hour ago like I told you."

"Never mind what you told us," the gruff voice retorted. "Go get us a lamp so we can see for ourselves."

"There's one right inside his room," Voss answered. "On the bureau."

"Yeah? Then come up here and make a light in it and bring it out to me," Voss was ordered. "Let him get by, fellers."

There was body movement outside, more boot-scraping and shuffling, then they heard bootsteps in Canavan's room, heard them head doorward again.

"Here y'are," they heard Voss say.

"Couple of you take a look inside," the gruff voice commanded. "Look under the bed and in the closet."

"Don't have any clothes closets here," Voss said.

"Then just under the bed, you fellers." There were more footsteps in Canavan's room. "High class joint you run here, Voss. I've seen better places and with clothes closets in every room, too, in flea-bitten towns in Mexico."

They heard Canavan's bed being moved across the uncovered floor.

"Not here, Rock!" a voice called.

"Y'see?" It was Voss again. "I told you he wasn't here."

"You told us, yeah, but that isn't good enough for us," the man with the thick voice replied. "We wanna know for sure. So we'll just have to search the rest of the place. Couple o' you men start down at the other end of the floor and look around. Some of you others take a look on the roof. Wouldn't put it past him to hide up there, figuring we wouldn't think of looking for him anywhere's else 'cept in his own room. Gimme that lamp, Kansas."

Boots thumped on the landing floor and passed the Lundy woman's room, and others came up to her door and stopped.

"Who's in here, Voss?"

"Number Four? A couple. Man and woman."

"We'll have a look anyway, just to be sure."

"Aw, don't do that!" Voss said quickly in mild protest. "What kind of a place will they think this is if you fellers bust in on them in the middle of the night?"

"Middle of the night, hell! It's only a little after nine, so chances are they haven't turned in yet."

"But they have," Voss argued. "You don't

see any light showing under their door, do you?"

"All the same..."

A heavy hand rapped on the door. When there was no answer, the door opened, and Canavan, not daring to move, opened one eye narrowly and stole a guarded look upward, saw thin rays of distant lamplight stab the darkness and dance over the ceiling. Ardis suddenly twisted around doorward, clutching the covers to her, and shielding her eyes with her bent arm and covering the better part of her face with it too, raised up a little and promptly screamed: "John! Wake up!"

Canavan, of course, did not stir. Ardis twisted around again, half sitting up, and pretended to be struggling with the covers as though she were trying to free herself of them, and crying at the same time a little frantically: "Where's your gun, John? Just let me get my hands on it, and I'll teach them to bust in on decent people when they're trying to get their well-earned rest! Oh, for pity's sake, I'm so tangled up! John!"

The way she held the covers to her while she continued her pretended struggle with them, the men in the doorway and those who had crowded up behind them and who were peering in over their mates' shoulders, saw her bared back, shoulders and arms and doubtless assumed she was completely naked. Proof of what they thought was the way one wide-eyed man's breath came hissing out of his open mouth.

"John!" Ardis cried again. "Wake up!"

"Aw, come on now, fellers," Voss protested again.

Reluctantly, Canavan was certain, the door was closed. Ardis got out of bed, ran to the door and turned the key in the lock. Then she spoke loudly so that the men outside the room could hear her: "Oh, you're finally awake, are you? I want you to get dressed right away, John. I want you to go find the sheriff and bring him back here with you."

Then in the same loud voice, and she made it sound a little tearful, she pretended to relate what had happened. Then she bent over Canavan and hissed at him: "Can you disguise your voice so they won't recognize it?"

"Yeah, I think so," he whispered back. "I can put on the meanest drawl you ever heard."

"Good. Tell me they've gone away and to go back to sleep."

"Right."

Canavan hoisted himself up on his elbows and drawled in a voice that was as unfamiliar to his own ears as it must have been to those who heard him: "Aw, now, honey. They've gone away, so why don't you go on back to sleep, huh? That's the good girl. Here, lemme cover you up. How's that? Aw-right? Good. Now just close your eyes and go on back to sleep. That's it. That's my good girl."

There was continued moving about outside the room, booted feet shuffling and striding and making the landing floor creak here and there when someone stepped on a warped board, and doors opening and closing. Then finally it stopped; there was no more opening and closing of doors, only a retreating past Ardis' door to the stairway.

"I think they're going," she whispered to Canavan. "Sounds like it, doesn't it?"

"Yeah."

There were heavy steps on the stairs, a massed descending of them. A hum of voices drifted upward from the tiny lobby and began to thin out and fade away as Harp's men crossed it and headed for the street. Then there was nothing, no sound, just silence.

Upstairs in Room Four, Canavan said in a musing tone: "Funny that of all the names you ever heard tell of, you picked John to holler to to wake up."

"It's such a common name, I suppose it was the first one I thought of," Ardis Lundy explained. Then as an afterthought she asked: "Oh, is that your name?"

"Uh-huh. John Joseph Canavan."

She was silent for a moment then she said: "I don't think you'll hear my name as often as you will John."

"No-o, I guess not. Don't think I've ever heard of anyone else named Ardis."

"I didn't know you knew my name," she said and there was surprise in her voice.

"Y'see I do though."

She had half turned to him; he could tell that because now he heard her slump down again on her back. They lay in silence for a long minute. Then both moved, and their hands, his right and her left, brushed. It was of course entirely accidental. But the touch of her hand against his stirred something inside of him. The darkness and the intimate closeness of her combined to arouse him. He reached out for her; his hand curled around her bare arm, tightened around it. He moved toward her.

"Don't," she whispered.

He was up on his knees then and bending over her, seeking her mouth with his eager lips. Someone came up the stairs and knocked on the door. Instantly Ardis pushed Canavan away and got out of bed.

"Y-es?" Ardis called, and Canavan thought he detected something of a quiver in her voice.

"Voss, Ma'm. They've gone, y'know. Thought you might want to know that as well as that the lunchroom's closed. So if you folks would like a little something to eat . . ."

"We would indeed, Mr. Voss, and it's awf'lly kind of you."

"Won't be much, y'know. Haven't got much. But it oughta do for now. So when you're ready, come right on downstairs."

He turned and walked away from the door. They heard him go down the stairs. Canavan moved across the bed, swung his long legs over the side and got up on his feet. Ardis stood a step or two away, a shadowy, motionless figure without a face.

"Thanks for doing what you did, Ardis," Canavan said quietly. "And I'm glad Voss came up when he did. That last part wasn't in the deal. I forgot myself, and I'm sorry. I'll go get cleaned up and meet you downstairs."

VI

Canavan rapped three times on Daws' back door, each time a little more insistently and with increasing impatience, too, before the stocky newspaper man appeared and admitted him. "What took you so long?" Canavan asked, stepping inside.

"I knew it was you," Daws said grumpily.

"Then why didn't you answer sooner?"

"Because I was busy," Daws retorted. "That's why." He grinned a little sheepishly and added: "I was doing my wash."

He bolted the door.

"Got some news for you," he said as he squared around to Canavan. "There won't be a single store open in Paradise tomorrow morning. Only places of business that will still be open will be the hotel and the stable."

They moved into the doorway between the back room and the office proper. Thin, dimmed lamplight played over the office floor but did not quite reach them. Hence they stood in the shadows.

"Swell. You really did a job of talking up to them, didn't you?"

Daws' rounded shoulders lifted a little.

"Oh, I don't know. Let's just say I gave the storekeepers something to think about. Actually, that's all I did. Plant the seed. The rest was up to them."

"If you want to be modest about it, all right. Anyway, we'll be coming to a showdown with Harp even sooner than I'd hoped."

"The sooner the better, I say. The sooner it happens, the sooner we'll be rid of him."

Canavan knew it wouldn't be that simple. But he offered no comment. Daws would find it out for himself, and in good time too.

"I looked for you to put in an appearance around six or so," the latter continued. "I waited a while before I went ahead and fixed some supper for myself. When you failed to show up, I began to wonder if something had happened to you. I was afraid your luck might have run out on you."

"Bet you didn't let your wondering interfere with your appetite though, did you?" Canavan chided him.

Daws bristled with indignation.

"With all that food around, what do you want me to do?" he demanded. "Let it stand and go bad and have to be thrown out?"

Canavan snorted.

"G'wan," he retorted. "No chance of anything like that happening around here. Bet you're stuffin' yourself right up to your ears. Look at you. No foolin' now, Daws. You're getting a belly on you already, and after only what, one day? I hate to think of what you'll look like after you've been shoveling grub into yourself for a month at the rate you've been doing it since you got your hands on Hoskins' stock. You'll probably be as wide as you are high."

Daws was still bristling; wisely though, he

held his tongue this time and didn't answer back.

"In case you're interested, and I don't think you are at all, we had supper with Voss."

"We?" Daws repeated. "Who's we?"

"Mrs. Lundy and me," Canavan replied, and he flushed uncomfortably under the quizzical look that Daws gave him.

"You don't say! Mrs. Lundy and you, huh?" The stocky man's thick eyebrows arched a bit. "That must have been real cozy."

"Why don't you wait till you know what happened and brought it about before you go letting your imagination run away with you?" Canavan demanded, still a little red-faced.

"All right. Then suppose you tell me so I'll know? I find it a little confusing trying to keep up with you."

"Oh, you do, huh?"

"Yes. One minute you don't want any part of her, and the next minute you're cozying up to her and having supper with her. Now if that isn't confusing to anyone who wants to understand and sympathize with you –"

"You think you can listen for a minute without putting in your two cents' worth?"

Daws grinned.

"Y-es, I think so."

"All right then."

Daws listened attentively, and without comment, to Canavan's recital of the episode at the hotel. Canavan, finishing, looked at him, and when Daws simply met his eyes, but said nothing, Canavan demanded: "Well?"

"Well, what?"

"Haven't you got anything to say?"

"What is there for me to say? I am curious though to know what you're going to do."

"You mean about Ardis?" Canavan asked, and he crimsoned again when Daws lifted another of his embarrassing looks to him. "Y'mean about Mrs. Lundy?"

"Yes."

"I don't know."

"I don't think you'll find many women who'd have done what she did for you tonight."

"I know, and that's the rub. That's what makes it so tough. Here I was all set to dump her. As a matter of fact, just a while before that, I told her I was finished with her. So she turns around and just about saves my hide for me and really puts me in debt to her. Doesn't it beat all how things work out?"

Daws wasn't at all helpful; he simply shrugged.

"The last thing I want right now is a woman..."

Canavan stopped himself. This time Daws hadn't anything to do with Canavan's flushing again. Canavan had only himself to blame, when he recalled all too guiltily what had nearly happened in the darkness of Ardis' room.

"I mean, to saddle myself with," he added hastily, and he hoped the squat little man with the steady gaze holding on him would not suspect that he, Canavan, hadn't told him everything. Then, because he was anxious to change the subject and avoid any further discussion of Ardis, since even the thought of her made him feel uncomfortable, he said: "Y'know, Daws, with the stores closed up, Harp and his crew will have to do something about feeding themselves. When they find they have to go somewheres else for food, don't expect when they get up on their horses and ride off that they won't be coming back. They'll be back, all right; and don't you think they won't. 'Course for how long that will go on depends on Harp, on how much dough he's got stashed away and how long he'll be able to keep handing it out to them to buy grub with. When he runs short, that'll be it. That's when his men will start riding off for good, looking around for another Paradise and another Judge Harp to take them in, feed them and protect them from the law. When that happens, he'll have to clear out too, when he sees he's been left high and dry. But not before. What's the nearest town to Paradise?"

"Primrose," Daws told him.

Canavan's lip curled.

"Nice names they give these flea-bitten places," he said scornfully. "Or isn't Primrose in the same fix Paradise let itself get into?"

"They have a school and a church in Primrose, so you can draw your own conclusions."

"What about the law in Primrose?"

"Things don't get out of hand there. They see to that."

"You don't say! Then maybe I owe Primrose an apology. For putting it in the same class with this lousy jerk-water town. How far is it from Paradise?"

"Oh, eighty or eighty-five miles."

"Which direction?"

"Northwestward."

"I'll lay you odds, Daws, that the minute Harp finds he's got himself a ghost town, he sends a wagon to Primrose for as much grub as the wagon can carry."

"And the way you see it, that will go on as long as his money lasts."

"Right."

"He's taken quite a lot of it out of Paradise."

"Yeah, guess he has. Couple o' hundred a week, the way I figure it."

"Four weeks to the month, and he's been here seven months. He's helped himself to several thousands of dollars."

"Uh-huh."

"Then we really haven't gained very much, have we, by persuading the storekeepers to close up? I mean, aside from cutting off Harp's income."

"We've gained that much. And now if we can do something to help him get rid of his money without letting him get anything in return for it, then we'll really have done something."

Daws wasn't particularly impressed with anything so remotely possible; he showed it by grunting and saying: "H'm."

"Since we came up with one way of hitting back at him, what's to stop us from coming up with still another?"

"Nothing, I suppose," Daws conceded. He suddenly peered hard at Canavan, then settling back on his heels, he said: "When you suggested the store-closing idea, I noticed a strange little gleam in your eye. It's there again. You've got something in mind, haven't you? What is it?"

Canavan grinned and answered: "Keep your shirt on and maybe I'll let you in on it. But first, Voss hasn't got much grub over at his place. Just about enough for tomorrow morning's breakfast, and a pretty skimpy breakfast it will be at that. And since he won't just be feeding himself –"

"Oh, yes ... there's that Lundy woman again."

"That's right. She has to eat too. Now if you'd quit stuffing yourself and hold your meals down to size and eat three times a day instead of every hour, you'd be able to spare them something too. That way what you've got stored away wouldn't take such a beating, and it would last."

Daws wore a darkening frown on his face.

"I made a sad mistake when I told you I'd brought Hoskins' stock over here," he said with an unhappy shake of his head.

"Want me to pay you for what you give them?"

"Who said anything about me wanting to be paid for it?"

"Nobody," Canavan admitted. "But I thought I'd better mention it in case that was what was bothering you."

Daws didn't answer. He glowered a bit, but he held his tongue.

"You want to know what I've got in mind?" Canavan asked. "Or don't you?"

"Oh, so that's it!"

"Huh?" Canavan looked at him blankly. "What do you mean?"

"I mean you want to trade with me."

"Hey, thanks for giving me the idea."

"Well, what's your plan?"

"First things first, Daws. Voss and Ardis gonna eat?"

"You don't think I'm going to let them go hungry, do you?"

"I don't know," Canavan answered.

Daws glowered again. "They'll eat," he said grumblingly.

"Good. I'm going to take a little ride for myself."

"In the direction of Primrose, I suppose."

"Wouldn't be at all surprised if that's where I wind up," Canavan said, a grin again parting his lips.

"What do you plan to do there?"

"Well, now, that's what I'm not sure about yet. But there must be something I can do, some way I oughta be able to mess things up for Harp."

"Go on."

"Well, take the wagon and the men who'll be driving it over to Primrose. Suppose the wagon should break down, or say something happens to the horses?"

"I think I'd like it better if something were to happen to the men," Daws said gravely.

"Poor, defenseless horses – I wouldn't want them to suffer for their owners' evil doings."

"Come to think of it, Daws, neither would I. So I guess it will have to be the men who run into hard luck."

"When do you plan to ride out?"

"I don't expect Harp to do anything till morning, after he finds everything's closed up on him. That's when he'll make his move. Being that I want to get the jump on him, have time to get myself set for whatever I decide to do, I think I'll head out for Primrose some time tonight."

"What about the Lundy woman?" Daws asked.

"What about her?"

"Suppose she asks for you, wants to know where you've gone and when you'll be back? What do you want me to tell her?"

"That you don't know," Canavan answered at once. "All you can tell her is that I had to go see somebody. But who that somebody is or where I had to go to see him, or when I figure to be back, you don't know because I didn't tell you."

"H'm," Daws said. He was thoughtfully silent for a moment, then he said: "From what you've told me about her, Canavan, I gather she's a rather persistent young woman."

"You don't think she'll be satisfied with that kind of answer?"

"No," Daws said bluntly. "I don't."

"I'm afraid that will have to be your problem, Daws, to handle the best way you can, yet without telling her anything. We've had one sample of me telling her something in confidence and having her spill it right out a minute after. So we can't take any chances with her."

Daws nodded understandingly and said: "There's just one thing more, Canavan."

"What's that?"

"You've admitted she has put you in a rather awkward position, and that you don't know what to do about it, or her. Right?"

"And how!"

"Well then, once you get going, what's to stop you from going on and never coming back here?" Daws asked boldly. "That would be the way out of this mess for you, and with my customary bad luck attending me, I'd probably wind up saddled with the lady. I'll be feeding her, and the next thing after that, and quite naturally too, I'll be expected to give her a place to stay. Particularly since she hasn't any money and boarding house mistresses expect to be paid for the rooms they rent out."

"You're getting 'way ahead of yourself

again, Daws. I don't think Voss will make any fuss if she stays on at his place for a while."

"Oh, you think he's in business for his health?"

"Nope," Canavan answered. "Nobody is. But being that he doesn't need her room for anybody else –"

"Regardless," Daws interrupted, "he'll still be expecting someone to assume her obligation for her, and when no one comes forward and offers to pay her room rent for her –"

"Hold it now, Daws," Canavan commanded. "This business of getting ahead of yourself must be catching. Another minute of listening to you and I'd be as bad off as you are. You're talking about this and that happening and all the while you're forgetting one important thing. That I'm coming back, and that none of that will have to happen."

"You're sure of that, are you?"

"Sure of what? Me coming back?"

"Yes."

"Only one thing can stop me," Canavan said evenly, "and I think you know what that is."

"A bullet from a Harp gun?"

Canavan nodded.

"Right. But being that I have plans for the

future, I aim to be awf'lly careful that I don't get in the way of a Harp slug."

Apparently that satisfied Daws for he did not pursue the voicing of his doubts and misgivings. Instead he asked: "Where've you got your horse?"

"Across the street in Lindfors' place," Canavan replied. He looked curiously at Daws. "Why?"

"You don't intend to ride boldly down the street and invite Harp's men to take a shot at you, do you?"

"The name's Canavan. Not Lundy."

Daws flushed a little.

"What's more," Canavan went on, "when I ride out, it won't be out the front way. It'll be out the back way. Then I'll swing wide around the town and when I'm clear of it, I'll head northwestward and that'll be that. No one will be any the wiser about me going."

There was no response.

"Anything else on your mind?" Canavan asked after a brief, moment-long silence. "You seem to be full of worries and doubts tonight. So if there's anything else bothering you, speak up, man, so we can settle it before I go. Wouldn't want to go off and leave you stewin' about something and have it spoil your appetite, you know."

Daws grinned rather sheepishly.

"Go on," he said. "Go get your horse and go about your business. And you'd better watch your step. I'm counting on you coming back here, you know."

Dawn broke over the range with a startling suddenness. A flickering candlelight appeared in the drab, grayish, empty sky, then steadied and burned evenly, then deepened and filled the sky with brightening light that awoke Canavan. He sighed deeply, a sort of long drawn-out wheezing, something of a thin hissing too, that ebbed out of him through his parted lips; he slumped over on his back. He grimaced when he shifted his blanketed body and felt a soreness in it.

"Sleeping in a bed sure spoils a man who's used to bedding down in the open," he thought to himself. "Even when it's only for a couple of nights. Softens him, spoils him for sleeping out again when he has to."

There was an uncomfortable chill in the air and a damp haze that rose up from the ground. It would be hours before the sun burned them away. For another minute or so he lay within the warm, protective folds of the blanket, then reluctantly he kicked it off and climbed stiffly to his feet. He stretched himself and grimaced again, stamped about till he felt a little freer in his movements.

There was a whinny and a grass-muffled beat of hoofs and Aggie trotted up to him, nuzzled his shoulder and was patted in return.

"All right now," Canavan told the mare, pushing her away when she sought to continue nuzzling him. "That's enough for now. We've got things to do, you know. So the sooner we get going, the better. Just gimme a couple of minutes to put something good and hot inside o' me and we'll be on our way. So g'wan now. Get outta here and let me get doing."

The mare backed off, wheeled around and trotted away. Canavan doubled up his blanket and draped it around his shoulders. He opened his saddlebags and hauled out his cooking implements, a bag of coffee and a good-sized package of bacon. He grinned inwardly when he recalled the wry expression on Daws' face when he had told him that he needed some supplies before he rode off to Primrose.

"Oh, fine," Daws had grumbled. "I sure did myself a favor taking Hoskins' stuff off his hands. But you know where the kitchen is and where I've got the stuff. So help yourself. Take enough though. No telling, y'know, whom you might run into on your travels. Some old friends possibly, and all of them probably half-starved. And I wouldn't want you to have to deny them anything and be anything but the perfect host. Goodness, no."

Canavan found a stretch of bare ground and built a fire there, and set about preparing his breakfast. By the time he had wolfed down a whole panful of crisp, curling bacon and had washed it down with two cups of steaming hot coffee, the sky had brightened even more and the chill had lessened. He noticed too that the ground haze had begun to dissolve. Aggie finished munching on a cropping of fresh young grass, looked over at him and whinnied, a sign that she was ready to go whenever he was; he grunted and got up again, stamped out the fire and saddled the mare. He rolled up his blanket and strapped it on in its usual place behind the saddle, washed the pot and the pan, the tin cup and plate with water from his canteen, and returned them to his saddlebag. Then he climbed up on Aggie's back and rode off westwardly. The mare wanted to stretch her legs and run; Canavan gave her her head for a few minutes, and when he pulled her up, slowed her to a lope, she protested loudly. He disregarded her snorting. After a while she gave up fighting for her head, but she continued to growl and grumble deep down in her throat. An hour passed, then two, and the sun broke through and spread its bright, dazzling warmth and cheer and Aggie forgot her grievance and whinnied happily as she pranced on. There was hill country ahead of them. The approach to the hills became increasingly rough, and Aggie did not protest when Canavan slowed her to a walk. Her hoofs drummed metallically when she plodded over the long, stony stretches of ground; she stopped a couple of times, raised her head and looked about her wonderingly, and Canavan, watching her, smiled. The trail he had been following led directly into the hills; wagon-wide it wound through a towering rock-walled pass that was about a mile long. Now the mare's hoofbeats echoed with an even sharper ringing clatter that caromed off the walls and climbed skyward where the brisk morning air caught it up and flung it about in all directions. Presently they emerged from the pass and into bright sunshine again and found themselves perched atop a gentle, grassy slope that spread away before them for miles. In fact, it seemed to roll on and lose itself in the distance.

Canavan halted Aggie after she had taken some half-a-dozen steps down the slope, and she looked around at him questioningly. Debating his course with himself, Canavan judged it to be about nine o'clock. If Harp had decided to dispatch a wagon to Primrose, this would be the time it would be leaving Paradise. The wagon, he was certain, wouldn't make the time that he had made. Hence his early start and Aggie's speed, far greater than the wagon team would be able to muster, would enable him to go through with the second of the two plans of action he had hit upon. He had already discarded two others, one because it was too risky and made its success dependent upon luck, the other because it was too impractical and left just a little too much to chance.

The first of the two acceptable plans called for him to waylay the oncoming wagon just as it wheeled into the pass. He was to pounce out upon it so suddenly, taking the men driving it so completely by surprise that capturing them would be fairly simple. Then disarming them and prodding them on ahead of him with his gun, he would herd them up into the hills, stop them when they came upon a cluster of screening rocks and boulders, tie them up and leave them there while he returned to the wagon. He would back it out of the pass, unhitch the horses pulling it and turn them loose and complete his mission by disposing of the wagon. But dissatisfaction with the last point made him waver. He hadn't been able to decide on how to do away with the wagon. If it was a farm wagon, and he was reasonably certain that it would be, disposing of anything so bulky and so cumbersome might give him more trouble than he could handle. All he knew was that he wouldn't be able to abandon it where it was left. If a second wagon was sent out, the sight of the first one standing by idly with neither its team nor the men assigned to it anywhere about would be sure to arouse the suspicions of the men driving the second one. Putting them on their guard would deprive him of the use of his best weapon, the element of surprise, and might well prove his undoing. And since he could not afford to take unnecessary chances, and there would be many of them if a shoot-out developed, he was concerned. That was why he finally decided against the plan, and why he chose the second one. And since it meant enlisting the aid of the Primrose sheriff in order to carry it off successfully, he lost no more time getting there.

He jerked the reins, and Aggie, eager to be on the move again and pawing the ground impatiently as an indication of it, responded instantly and loped down the slope. This time Canavan did not try to hold her in check. He eased his grip on the reins and the fleet mare bounded away over the widespreading carpet of lush green that leveled off before them. And later on when the hard-running mare slackened her speed, it was of her own doing, not Canavan's. And when he felt that she had loafed long enough he did not urge her to go on. He was content to leave the pace-setting and the speed to her.

It was about noon when she suddenly sensed the nearness of water and she trumpeted the news of it to Canavan who rose up in the stirrups and, hand-shading his eyes, confirmed it. A couple of hundred yards away and somewhat to the north was a narrow, crookedly running brook with a single tree, a shade tree, arching its branches over it. They came drumming up to it minutes later. Canavan dismounted and as he plodded down the short bank to the tree Aggie made her way down to the water. Canavan eased himself down in the grass under the tree and slumped back; after a while he struggled up into a sitting position and, sitting hunched over, watched the mare frolic about. She was standing in the water and splashing it about noisily and happily, and swishing her long tail and slapping it against her legs. When Canavan felt that she had had enough, he trudged down to the water's edge and said: "All right, Aggie. Let's go."

She gave no sign that she had heard him.

"Aggie," he said again, sternly this time, and she turned her head and stole what she must have thought was a guarded and therefore undetected look at him. "I said, let's go. Now you heard me and don't try to make out you didn't. Come outta there."

She was motionless for another moment, then she wheeled around and stepped up on the bank and shook herself. When she stood still again, Canavan climbed up into the saddle. Aggie carried him across the stream, plodded up the gently sloping bank, topped it and loped off with him.

The early afternoon passed uneventfully, then it was three o'clock, four, five, and still they pushed on. Dusk had come on when Canavan finally pulled up and dismounted. He unsaddled Aggie and left her to her own devices while he set about preparing his supper, another meal of bacon and coffee. When he had finished eating, he lay back in the grass propped up on one elbow. Darkness came on, deepening steadily, and reluctantly Canavan forced himself up. He washed and dried and put away the things he had used, took note of the fact that he had cut deeply into the bacon and the coffee. He would have to remember to replenish his supply of both of them when he reached Primrose. He whipped open his blanket and spread it out over a grassy patch of ground, stamped out his fire and rolled up in the blanket. A breeze came up and rustled the grass. Then another one came sweeping up, a far stiffer one than the first, and when it flung dust about, Canavan burrowed deeper in the blanket, reached up for an end and flipped it over his head and face. A little later on when Aggie trotted up, bent over him and nudged him, there was no response. Canavan was asleep. The mare turned away.

Canavan was up at dawn, and on his way again half-an-hour later. The dawn light had just begun to brighten a little when he heard faint hoofbeats somewhere off in the distance. Despite the muffling grass, he could hear them coming steadily closer. He pulled up at once and twisted around, scanned the awakening range alertly for a sign of the oncoming rider. The hoofbeats swelled and presently a horseman appeared, came loping up from the south and, spotting Canavan, yelled something that sounded like "Hi, there, partner!" Canavan acknowledged the greeting with a friendly wave of his hand. Passing him at about a hundred feet away, the man rode on in a northerly direction as Canavan watched, and soon disappeared from sight.

It was late afternoon when Canavan, so

saddle-stiff that even the barest movement on his part was a painful effort, wheeled weary-legged Aggie into Primrose and walked her down the street till they came to the sheriff's office. Reining in at the curb in front of the place, Canavan sat motionlessly for a minute or so, then with a deep sigh, climbed down stiffly, grimacing. He patted the head-bowed mare's rump and stepped up on the walk, trudged up to the door and tried it. It was locked. He knocked on it a couple of times and looked keenly disappointed when there was no answer. There were bootsteps on the planked walk and as he turned in their direction, a man came tramping up and said: "If you're looking for the sheriff, Mister, you'll have to come back again."

"Yeah? When?"

"Oh, say in a couple of days."

"You mean he's gone off somewhere?"

"That's right."

"That's swell," Canavan complained. "I've come eighty-five miles to see him and just about wore myself out and maybe ruined my horse doing it, and he isn't around and won't be for a couple of days. That's real swell."

The townsman, a rather elderly and seedy-looking individual with a week's growth of beard on his lined face, shrugged, but he made no comment.

"The sheriff got a deputy?" Canavan asked hopefully.

"Yeah, sure," was the reply. "Got himself a good one, too."

"Well, where'll I find him?"

The man grinned, revealing a toothless lower jaw.

"Where you'll find the sheriff, Mister," he said stepping around Canavan. "They went off together."

VII

It was a day later. A big, heavy, canvas-roofed farm wagon drawn by a team of shaggy, wearied-looking horses rumbled over the ribbony stretch of road that led to Primrose. It was open country, as flat and as level as a tableland. Hence the two men who were riding on the driver's seat could see the hazy outline of the town despite the five miles that lay between it and them. One of the men was the swarthy Vasco who carried his shattered and thickly bandaged right wrist in a sling, and who kept reaching across his body every little while with his left hand, practicing getting his gun out of the holster that was thong-tied around his right thigh. At first he had abandoned the holster and had taken to wearing his gun thrust down inside the waistband of his pants. But it had proved uncomfortable and he had tied on the holster in its usual place. His companion was Jake Bright, another of Judge Harp's followers. Bright was a long, lean, angular, slope-shouldered individual, possessor of the biggest nose and ears that anyone had ever seen on a man, and a mouth that was so sharply and contrastingly small that it was lost under his nose. His appearance belied the fact that he was a killer, a cold and deliberate one too. He drove the wagon while Vasco rode next to him in the capacity of guard although both men knew there was no actual need for one.

It was due to Harp that Vasco was participating in the Primrose mission. The judge had neither sympathy nor understanding for anyone in his organization who failed to carry out an assignment. The man who had flung the wild shot at Canavan and who had then fled in fright had already been chased out of town at Harp's insistence. Marve Russell had failed.

However, he had paid with his life for his failure, so Harp was satisfied. Vasco too had failed. But because he was still alive, he had to bear the brunt of Harp's scornful glances and biting remarks. Since Vasco was not the kind who could stand up under that sort of treatment, he sought escape from his tormentor even for only a brief time. When he heard that a wagon was to be sent to Primrose, he seized upon it for it provided him with the excuse he needed.

But he was a little surprised when Harp consented so readily to his going along with Bright. He thought the judge considered him one of his most reliable men, felt that despite his wound which made it practically impossible for him to do anything physical, his mere presence helped Harp maintain his feeling of security. He felt too that his over-all record of performance under the judge's banner had made his berth with Harp secure, and refused to believe that his one failure had really soured Harp on him. When his wrist was better, and a week's time would make a noticeable improvement in it he was sure, he would show Harp and any of the others who had begun to wonder about him a thing or two. He had no way of knowing that the judge had been casting about for a way in which to dispose of him, that once a man was disabled, the judge had no further use for him, and that by his request for permission to accompany Bright to Primrose, he had furnished Harp with an answer to his problem.

Vasco hadn't expected the trip to be a comfortable or pleasurable one, and it wasn't. Whenever the wagon's big wheels hit a rough spot in the road, or he was jounced unexpectedly, he winced. And whenever that happened, and he wasn't going through the motions of reaching for his gun, he would hastily cradle the elbow of his injured arm in the protective hollow of his cupped left hand in an effort to ease the jarring and painful effect of the jouncing. Bright glanced at him from time to time, but he made no comment. And Vasco endured the pain without complaint.

Then Primrose was suddenly directly ahead of them, and minutes later they were wheeling into the town and the big wagon was rumbling downstreet.

"Hey," Bright remarked after ranging a quick look about him. "This place is all right. Y'know? Helluva lot bigger and nicer than Paradise."

Vasco grunted and shifted himself a little. The hard wooden seat was anything but comfortable, and after three days of it, Vasco had had his fill of it.

"I was just thinking," he said. "Took us nearly three whole days to make it here from Paradise. Another day to rest up the horses for the trip back, then three days more after that to do it in. That comes to seven days, a week, all told."

"Uh-huh. Looks like a church down at the corner, doesn't it?"

"So what?" Vasco demanded.

"Nothing," Bright answered calmly. "Just mentioned it. O-oh, and there's a school. Must be a lot o' folks here in Primrose raising families."

Vasco frowned.

"Hurray for them," he said grumpily. "If Harp has to wait seven days before he gets something to eat, he'll be dead of starvation by the time we get back to Paradise."

"He doesn't aim to wait at all. Guess you didn't hear what he was gonna do meanwhile."

"What was that?"

"Heard him tell Mike Hoban to get the crew together and bust into every store in town and clean it out of everything that could be eaten."

"O-oh, yeah?"

"And if that didn't turn up enough grub to

hold him and the others till we get back," Bright continued, "he said Mike was to go see the cattlemen and get them to supply the grub."

"That store down the street," Vasco said, pointing with his left hand. "The one with the sign that says —"

" 'Gebhardt's General Store'? That the one Harp said for us to get the stuff from?"

"Yeah."

"Mister Gebhardt doesn't know it yet," Bright added in a musing tone, "but I'll bet the order we're gonna give him will top any he's ever had before. And he oughta be tickled to death with it because it's gonna be for cash. No book business and then having to go chase after the customer to collect his dough."

Vasco had no comment to offer. He felt belittled and couldn't understand why Harp hadn't entrusted him rather than Jake Bright with the money for the foodstuffs they were to buy. After all, the angular and loose-jointed Bright was a comparative newcomer as far as he was concerned, admittedly the owner of a rather awing reputation, but as yet untried and unproved as a Harp follower. He had already begun to resent Bright, had even started to build a dislike for the man. That it was all of Harp's doing and none of Bright's, and that the latter was simply following the judge's instructions, apparently never occurred to him. Perhaps subconsciously he was aware of it; if that was so, his frown indicated that he wasn't letting it interfere with his building resentment of the man. Bright guided the team over toward the low curb and drove along it till they came abreast of the general store. Then he brought the horses to a full stop, pulled back hard on the handbrake, and slumped back in his seat. Vasco leveled a look at him. Bright met his eyes and grinned back at him.

"I'm beat," Bright announced. "And I don't mind telling you that." Vasco grunted. "You wanna know something else, Vasco? I'm damned glad we have to lay over for a day. Because once I hit the sack in that hotel down near the corner, I'm gonna sleep clear around the clock. I don't know what you aim to do meantime. But you sure know what I'm gonna do."

He looped the loose ends of the reins around the brake and climbed down. Half-turned toward the store, he stood at the wheel and watched Vasco move himself over the worn-surfaced seat, turn himself around and carefully climb down too. Then with Bright hitching up his levis and leading the way, they trooped into the store. Otto Gebhardt, a short, heavily built and graying man, wearing a frayed string bowtie, sleeve garters and an apron that was too long for him and which he had to wear unusually high up, almost around his chest, to prevent its getting underfoot, was at the shadowy rear, sweeping the floor, and plying his broom with thoughtful industry. He looked downward when he heard entering footsteps; when he saw the two men, he propped the broom against an empty, up-ended box and trudged forward. He nodded a greeting to them and took his place behind the counter.

"That apron you're wearing is kinda long for you, isn't it, partner?" Bright asked as he came up to the counter and thumbed his dust-streaked hat up from his forehead. "The way it was flappin' around your feet, I expected it to trip you up with every step." Gebhardt didn't answer. Bright produced a folded sheet of paper, unfolded it and slapped it on the counter. There were two columns of items listed on the sheet. "There y'are," he said, pushing it across the counter. "Probably the biggest order for stuff you ever got. Now look. We won't be pulling out've here till around this time tomorrow. So meanwhile you get the stuff together and put it aside till we come back for it. Oh, don't forget to have a bill ready too. Got to show the boss where his money went."

Gebhardt picked up the sheet and ran his eye over the listed items.

"This will run into money," he said after a moment, raising his eyes to Bright.

"That's all right."

"Where you men from?"

"That make any difference to you?" Bright wanted to know, putting his hand on his gun butt with a significant deliberateness that wasn't lost on the storekeeper. "Long as you get your money?"

Gebhardt flushed.

" 'Course not," he said quickly.

"That's what I figured," Bright said dryly.

"I didn't mean anything by it, Mister," Gebhardt hastened to assure him. "It was just that I couldn't remember ever seeing you and your friend here 'round Primrose before. And I wondered. But that's all."

"Forget it. Just treat us right and you'll see more of us and more of our money," Bright responded, and turned to Vasco. "What d'you say? You set? Then let's go."

"Stable's down the street a ways, Mister," Gebhardt called after them as Bright led the way doorward, "if you want to put up your team overnight. Down the street and across. And you might tell whoever's there that

I sent you and for him to put it on my bill."

Bright didn't look back. He simply waved his hand in acknowledgment as he went out.

It was the following day. The big wagon with its team of horses looking more alert was drawn up at the low planked curb outside the general store. Inside Gebhardt was behind the counter, bent over it, totaling up the bill for which Jake Bright, leaning cross-legged against the counter, was patiently waiting. Vasco, with his back turned, was standing idly about midway between Bright and the front door, staring streetward rather dejectedly. Earlier he had tried his injured wrist, tried it by flexing the fingers of his right hand and then attempting to ball his hand into a fist. The result had been anything but encouraging. A spasm of pain had shot through his wrist and arm, and he had cursed bitterly.

Sunlight suddenly showed at the shadowy rear when the back door opened and thin rays played over the dusty floor a step or two inside the doorway. There was movement at the rear, a footstep, and a loose floorboard creaked dismally. Gebhardt heard it and so did Bright. The former looked up wonderingly; the latter uncrossed his legs and straightened up, turned his head and ranged his gaze after the storekeeper's. Gebhardt stared hard. Bright stiffened, but that was all. There was a gun holding on him, and it forbade movement of any kind on his part. When a tall figure with a level gun in his hand came forward from the rear, Gebhardt gulped and swallowed hard and made a wry face.

"Reach, Mister," Canavan said curtly to Bright. "And turn around."

Bright looked at him obliquely; when Canavan gestured with his gun, Bright turned slowly, raised his hands slowly too. Canavan came swiftly across the intervening space, glided up behind Bright and, digging his gun muzzle into the lanky Jake's back, yanked the latter's gun out of his holster and promptly stepped back again.

"You, Vasco."

Wallowing in his unhappy thoughts, the dark-faced Vasco apparently had not heard Canavan.

"Vasco!"

Startled, Vasco jerked around. Just as Gebhardt had done, he stared hard when he saw Canavan and saw the latter's gun gaping at him. Stepping wide around Bright, Canavan came up to Vasco, caught him by the arm, spun him around and lifted the gun out of his holster, stuck it in his belt next to Bright's, and backed off again.

"All right, you two," he commanded. "Let's go."

Still holding his gun on them, he backed to the doorway and waited there for them to come toward him; when they did, he moved aside to permit them to pass, turned after them and followed them out. On the walk, he prodded Bright with his gun and forced him to fall in at Vasco's side, and herded them downstreet. Passersby stopped when they came along and quickly crossed the walk to the curb or backed against the nearest building to give them ample passing room. They looked wonderingly at Canavan's captives and then at him. He stared back stonily. As they neared the sheriff's office, two horsemen came loping up the street, slowed their mounts and wheeled in to the hitch rail in front of the sheriff's place. One man, a lean, wiry, sun-bronzed individual with an edge-tarnished metal star pinned to the buttoned-down flap of his shirt pocket and a butt-jutting gun riding high on his right hip, swung down at once, flipped the reins to his dismounting companion and stepped up on the walk.

"Just a minute now," he commanded, holding up his hands and barring the way to Vasco and Bright. "What's going on here?"

Canavan stepped around Vasco and stood facing him and Bright, and with his gun still leveled at them, said, head turned to the lawman: "Got a couple of customers for you, Sheriff."

"You don't say! Drumming up trade for me, huh? And who are you?"

"Name's Canavan. But I think you'll find their names a lot more interesting than mine if you'll let us come inside and wait while you go over your wanted lists."

The sheriff's companion, a younger man, a little taller and a little huskier than average, had unlocked and opened the door to the office, and now he was standing in the doorway, straddling the threshold strip, waiting and looking on. Canavan glanced at him. He wore a star that was even more tarnished than the sheriff's, wore it where the sheriff wore his. The latter looked around; when he saw that the door was open, he turned on his heel and, slanting across the walk to the office, called over his shoulder to Canavan: "All right, Mister. Bring them in."

Motioning with his gun and disregarding the glowering looks that Vasco gave him, Canavan herded his prisoners into the office ahead of him. The sheriff, rounding the desk that stood cater-cornered between the street door and the connecting door that opened into the usual back room, seated himself at his desk, squared back in his chair, looked up and said: "All right, you men." He looked first at Bright. "What's your name, Mister?"

"Smith," Bright answered calmly. "John Smith."

"Huh," Canavan said scornfully.

The sheriff frowned at him, then he leveled a questioning look at Vasco.

"And you, Mister? What's your name?"

"It's Vasco," Canavan said before the dark-faced man could answer for himself. "And that big-nosed buzzard's name isn't Smith any more than it's mine or yours. Dig out those lists, Sheriff, and I know damned well you'll find Vasco's name on at least one of them. As for him," indicating Bright with a curt nod, "you don't have to know his right name. Just look through the lists till you come to a description that fits him, and that'll be that."

The sheriff moved back in his chair and tried to open the center desk drawer; he tugged and tugged at it but it refused to open. The deputy who had closed the door after Canavan had entered the office, and who had been standing with his back against it, a little spread-legged and with his thumbs hooked in his gunbelt, watched the sheriff struggle with the unyielding drawer for another minute, then he said: "Trying to force it won't open it, Buck. Must be something stuck in there. We'll have to get Toby Sims to come over after a while and open it." Then he added: "I'd go after him now only I know it wouldn't be any good. That boss o' his won't give him even one lousy minute's time off during the day. So we'll have to wait till he gets through working, and that'll be after six."

The sheriff lifted his eyes, met Canavan's, shrugged and said: " 'Fraid we won't be able to get a look at those lists for a while now, Mister. Like Barney just said, not till after six."

"That where you keep your lists?" Canavan asked. "In that middle drawer?"

"Yeah. Why?"

"How about giving me a crack at that drawer? You just let me get at it with a knife and –"

"Nope," the sheriff said firmly. "I don't aim to let anybody go bustin' up county property that I'm responsible for. We'll just sit tight till six o'clock, till Sims can come over and open it for us. He's a locksmith and he'll know how to open it without bustin' it up any."

"H'm," Canavan said darkly.

The sheriff sat back again in his chair. He looked up at Bright, then at Vasco, and asked, turning his gaze back to Canavan: "What'd these two do? What are you charging them with?"

"With every crime in the book," Canavan replied. "They belong to the Harp gang over at Paradise."

"Paradise?" the sheriff repeated. "That isn't my territory, Mister. I work Primrose, the town and the county, but that's all. I can't touch anything outside the county line. They do anything over here?"

"They haven't been here long enough for that," Canavan said curtly.

"The point is, Mister, if they didn't do anything in Primrose, then I can't hold them. What they've done elsewhere . . ."

"You mean you can't take in somebody who's hightailing it from the law of another state?" Canavan demanded.

"If I can prove it, sure."

"And if you know that somebody is part of a gang that's raising holy hell in the next town to you . . . ?"

"Mister, why don't you go find yourself a marshal and tell him what's bothering you? A marshal can go anywhere, across state lines, anywhere, and he can do whatever he thinks is right and nobody can say a word. He represents the gover'ment and Washington gives him a pretty free hand. But when it comes to a local lawman," the sheriff shook his head, "his hands are tied."

Bright coughed behind his upraised hand.

"Sheriff," he said, and the lawman's eyes shifted away from Canavan and held questioningly on Bright. "Sheriff, all right for me to say something?"

"Yeah, sure. Talk up."

"Well, it's this way, Sheriff. We came here from Paradise to buy a lot o' grub to take back with us. Gebhardt up the street's got everything we ordered ready for us. All we've got to do is pay him for the stuff, load it into our wagon that's waiting in front of his place, and get going. That's what we've done to your town. Brought good money into it. We've got a long ways to go. Three whole days, maybe even four being that the horses will be pulling a load instead of an empty wagon, before we get back to Paradise. So we'd sure like to get squared away with Gebhardt, get loaded up and head out. If we have to wait around till sundown – and no matter what Canavan says you won't find our names on any wanted list – it'll mean we'll be losing another day because we won't be able to drive in the dark and we'll have to lay over till tomorrow. Now how about it, Sheriff? What do you say?"

"You let them go, Sheriff," Canavan warned the lawman, "and you'll be layin' yourself wide open for trouble."

"Mister," the sheriff said evenly. "I don't like it when somebody tries to tell me what to do or what not to do. I'm the one who decides. This is my job and I make the decisions that have to do with it. I've had the job twelve years now. And being that I'm still wearing this," he fingered his tarnished star, "I guess I've been making the right ones all these years. You two fellers clear out of here, get your stuff out of Gebhardt's, and start rolling."

"Right, Sheriff," Bright responded. "And thanks." He turned, met Canavan's angry eyes, smiled into them tauntingly, and held out his hand. "My gun, if you don't mind, MISTER Canavan."

Canavan frowned, eased Bright's gun out of his belt and clapped it into the man's hand. He did the same thing with Vasco's. The two men holstered their guns and marched out. Canavan gave his levis an angry hitching-up, gave the sheriff a hard look, and turned doorward.

"Just a minute, Canavan," the sheriff said. Canavan stopped a stride or two from the door and looked back at him. "No point in you goin' off mad. How about letting me buy you a glass of beer?"

"You can't buy me anything," Canavan flung back at him, yanked open the door and stalked out.

He halted on the walk, looked upstreet and spied Vasco and Bright entering the general store. He sauntered out to the curb shortly and stood there, still looking up the street. After a few minutes, Vasco emerged dragging a rope-bound wooden box behind him. He hauled it out to the curb, unchained and dropped the wagon's tail-gate, and after something of a struggle due to the fact that he was restricted to the use of only one hand, managed to lift the box and get it into the wagon. Then he tramped back into the store. After that it developed into a steady procession, first Vasco, then Bright, and in between times, Gebhardt himself, each carrying things out of the store and loading them in the wagon. Finally, after some fifteen minutes, the loading job was done. Vasco, waiting on the walk near the wagon, started to hoist himself up to the driver's seat when Bright, tucking a folded square of paper in his shirt pocket, appeared in the doorway, looked up and called to Vasco, stopping him. Bright came striding across the walk and Vasco turned to face him. Canavan, watching, wished he could have heard their conversation. Had he been close enough, he would have heard Vasco ask as Bright joined him: "What's the matter, Jake?"

And he would have heard the lean, angular Bright answer: "I'm kinda disappointed."

Then: "Huh? What d'you mean you're disappointed? Disappointed in what?"

"I'm disappointed in you."

"In me? What did I do?"

"I didn't need you along on this trip. You knew that, I knew it and the judge knew it."

"So what? If the judge didn't want me to go, he would've said so, wouldn't he?"

"That's the point, Vasco. He wanted you to go."

"Then what are you driving at?"

"Like I said, Harp wanted you to go. But he doesn't want you to come back. I've been waiting for the best time to tell you that. Then I got to thinking that maybe I wouldn't have to tell you. That maybe because of the way he'd been riding you, layin' it into you good, that once we got here, you'd decide for yourself that you'd had enough of him and that you didn't want any more, and that you'd made up your mind not to go back to Paradise. Instead, you were gonna look around for somebody else to tie up with. That's what I've been hoping for."

"Hold it a minute, Jake."

"Yeah?"

"Harp tell you that himself, that he doesn't want me to come back, or is that something you . . . ?"

"Told me that himself."

"Why, the son-uva-bitch! So that's the way he pays me back for doing his dirty work for him all these months! And believe me, there was plenty of it to do too. I get hurt doing a job for him, and because I'm liable to be laid up with this busted wrist for another couple o' weeks, and he'll have to feed me and keep me going till I'm able to sling a gun for him again, he wants to get rid of me. The dirty, no-good son-uva-bitch! Wait, Jake. You'll get the same kind of deal from him when your turn comes. I know because I've seen others get it from him too. But they never did the jobs for him that I did. So I never figured he'd hand me this kind of deal."

Bright held his tongue.

"I'm not pulling out just yet, Jake. Not till I've told him face-to-face what I think of him, the lousy bastard."

"I wish you wouldn't, Vasco."

"Why not? What's it got to do with you? You can tell him that you told me, but that

I wouldn't take it from you and that I said I wanted him to tell me."

Canavan saw Vasco turn again and climb up and settle himself on the wide seat. Then he saw Bright climb up too, move past Vasco and take his place next to him and unwind the reins from around the handbrake. A minute later the wagon stirred and moved. It lurched away from Gebhardt's, the iron rims of its big wheels scraping the low wooden curb. It swung around, straightened out and rumbled up the street. Canavan's gaze ranged after it. He saw it reach the corner. When it took the eastward road that led back to Paradise, he turned away.

It was two days later and thirty-eight miles from Primrose. The ground fell away sharply on both sides of the wagon-wide road with rocky ravines flanking it. There had been little conversation between Bright and the bitter-eyed, tight-mouthed Vasco. Each was absorbed by his own thoughts. Hence the only sounds came from the horses, from the steady, almost rhythmic plod of their hoofs, from the wagon, from the creak of its body and the crunch of its wheels as they ground stone and shale into the roadbed, and from the creaking harness. Bright suddenly brought the team to a stop. Vasco looked up.

"What's the matter?" he asked, lifting a questioning look to Bright. "What did you stop here for?"

Bright sat back. " 'Fraid this is as far as you're going, Vasco," he replied.

"Huh?" Vasco stared at Bright. "Y'mean you're dumping me 'way out here, in the middle of nothing?"

The lanky man's right arm suddenly jerked backward. His gun appeared in his right hand. The fire-burned muzzle held on a line with Vasco's stomach.

"Gave you your chance back in Primrose," Bright told him. "But you wouldn't take it. Get down."

"I'll be goddamned! I never thought you'd pull anything like this on me, Jake. If you didn't want me to go back with you, why didn't you say so while we were still in Primrose? I'd have found some other way of getting back to Paradise without you. But to dump me out cold in the middle of nowhere –"

"Get down, Vasco," Bright repeated. "Must be something of Harp's rubbed off on you."

Bright's gun came up the barest bit and steadied again.

"All right, Jake," Vasco said. "I'll get down. But I won't forget this. And when I get around to squaring up with Harp, I won't forget I've got some squaring up to do with you too."

He climbed down. Still covering him with his gun, Bright climbed down too. Vasco gave him a glowering look, turned and started to walk back in the direction from which they had come. He was probably a dozen feet from Bright when the latter's gun suddenly roared. Vasco gasped and stumbled, staggered and tottered a little; he steadied himself with an effort, straightened up too, reached across his body and managed to get his gun out of his holster. He turned stiffly. Just as he raised his gun, Bright shot him twice more. The impact of the bullets slamming into Vasco's body rocked him, spun him halfway around, and his legs began to buckle under him.

"You lousy..."

He didn't finish. Blood gushed from his mouth and choked off his words. He put out his hand as though he were seeking something to grasp and hang onto when Bright blasted him, emptied his gun into him. Vasco tottered brokenly and dropped his gun. He toppled backward off the edge of the road and plummeted downward. His bullet-riddled body struck a big rock and slid off its smooth, slanting surface and fell limply between it and another rock. Striding up to the spot from which Vasco had fallen, Bright peered down at him. When Vasco failed to move, Bright appeared to be satisfied that he was dead, stepped back and reloaded his gun, and started back to the wagon. He stopped and wheeled around, retraced his steps to where Vasco's gun lay and kicked it off the road, then he trudged away. He drove off shortly. He stood up and looked back just once. The road behind him was deserted. Sinking down again he flipped the loose ends of the reins over the horses' backs; when they did not respond, he lashed them a couple of times. They got moving, picked up speed, and the wagon lurched from side to side. But after a few minutes the horses slackened their pace and resumed their steady jogging. It produced less jouncing and made for easier riding, and Bright, aware of it, did not urge them on again. Instead he slumped back, eased his grip on the reins and permitted the horses to make and maintain their own pace.

It was nearly sundown when Bright came to a rock- and boulder-lined stretch of roadway that was rough and stony. He sat up, pulled back on the lines and slowed the team to a walk. When the horses suddenly stopped, he looked up wonderingly, raised up a little, too, and peered over their heads. A couple of good-sized rocks had rolled into the road, blocking it. Frowning, Bright curled the reins around the handbrake and climbed down.

"Hold it, Mister," a voice said somewhere behind him and he stiffened. He recognized the voice. It was Canavan's. He tensed a little. "Fell for the oldest trick in the book, didn't you? Get your hands up. And don't try 'ny tricks. I'm suspicious by nature and I've got an awf'lly itchy trigger finger, and I'm liable to misunderstand and shoot first and wonder afterward if you were really up to something or if I read the signs all wrong. G'wan now. Reach."

Slowly Bright's hands began to climb, the left one just the barest bit faster than the right. He spun around suddenly, his right hand clawing for and coming up with his gun. He fired from the hip. But Canavan, watching him alertly and sensing what the man would do, side-stepped instantly, and fired too. Bright's bullet, instinctively aimed at the spot on which Canavan had been standing, failed to find the target. But Canavan's found its mark. It struck Bright in the right arm, numbing it, and Bright winced and dropped his gun. He glowered at Canavan and hunched a little. When he suddenly bent and lunged and sought to retrieve his gun with his left hand, Canavan shot him in the left arm. Bright tottered momentarily, steadied himself with an effort and, raising up again, stood glaring at Canavan with his sloping shoulders even more rounded than usual and his arms brought together limply in front of him. The fire-blackened muzzle of Canavan's gun gaped at him tauntingly and seemed to be urging him, goading him in fact, to make another attempt to snatch up his own gun, and he looked down at it and appeared to be debating his chances.

"I found your side-partner," he heard Canavan say and he looked up at him. "Probably would have passed him by 'cept for the blood I spotted in the road. That's what led me to him. You gave it to him good, didn't you? Four times in the front and twice in the back. But I'll bet you shot him in the back first, didn't you?"

Bright's eyes burned, but he held his tongue and stole another look at his gun.

"So I lit out after you," Canavan went on, and again Bright lifted his eyes to him. "Circled around and came up ahead of you and waited for you to come along. Wondered if you'd fall for that old trick of dumping rocks in the road in order to stop you and make you climb down so I could get to you, or if you'd suspect something was up and make a break for it. But you were so sure you were getting away with killing Vasco, you fell for it just the way I hoped you would. Only now there isn't anyone here for me to turn you over to, no law in Paradise and a lame-brained sheriff back in Primrose. So I guess I'll have to be the law."

Bright's lip curled. "Huh," he said scornfully.

"Got anything to say for yourself?"

"Yeah," Bright fairly spat him. "Go t'hell."

"I find you guilty of murder, Mister," Canavan said evenly.

Bright suddenly sank down on his knees. He curled both hands around his gun and hunched over it. Then slowly he eased back on his haunches and raised the gun with his two hands. Higher and higher it came up. Finally, it stopped. As he tried to trigger it, Canavan's gun roared with an echoing fury. Slug after slug tore into Bright's body. He was whipped about, then blown over backward and dumped brokenly in the roadway.

VIII

Christopher Daws sat head-bowed and nodding at the lamp-lighted table in his kitchen. His clasped hands were in his lap. An opened book lay on the table almost directly below his bobbing head. On the side wall opposite him, an old clock ticked off the time. Daws awoke suddenly, with a body-jerking start and looked about him. Then, with equal suddenness he became aware of a stiffness in the back of his neck, and he grimaced and rubbed the sore spot, stopped for a moment to look up at the clock. When he saw the time, a minute short of midnight, he shook his head, climbed stiffly to his feet and trudged downstairs. He bolted the street door to his office and turned away, then stopped and turned back to put his eye to a crack between the boards he had nailed up over the shattered front window. The street was steeped in deep darkness and hushed. He wheeled around instantly when he heard a quick and impatient but guarded rap on the back door. Swiftly he padded across the floor to the darkened office to answer it. Through the back room's uncovered window he glimpsed a tall, shadowy figure outside. He unlocked the door, opened it and backed with it. Canavan stepped inside and Daws closed the door after him and locked it again, and followed him into the office where they stopped and faced each other.

"So you did come back after all," Daws began.

"Told you I would," Canavan retorted. "Didn't I?"

"Y-es," Daws admitted. "You did. But after a couple of days went by, I began to think you might have changed your mind and that we'd never see you again." Something that had weight and heft to it thumped on the floor. "What . . . what was that?"

"What d'you think? A sack full o' money maybe? It's grub. Bacon, coffee and sugar. Damned thing must weigh a good hundred pounds, maybe even more than that, if it weighs an ounce. I musta thought I was a pack horse, luggin' that much weight around with me. But that's beside the point. I couldn't see it go to waste, and even though I know you don't need the stuff –"

"Oh, don't we though! For your information, my uninformed friend, we haven't had a cup of coffee in three days now."

"Huh? How come? What happened to all that stuff you had put aside, the stuff you got from Hoskins?" Canavan wanted to know. Then before Daws could answer, Canavan added: "I know you were stuffin' yourself like there was no tomorrow when I left here, but you couldn't have gone through everything that fast."

"Again for your information, MISTER Canavan," Daws said, and his voice was freighted with sarcasm. "I had nothing to do with what happened to our food supply. The morning after you left here, your good friend, Judge Harp –"

"Hold it, Daws," Canavan commanded, interrupting him. "I think you'd better start all over again, and stick to the facts. Harp's no friend of mine, and if anyone knows that, you do. He might like to be. But he isn't because I'm kinda choosy."

"Sorry," Daws said, but his tone belied his apology. "As I started to say when I was so, we-ll, when I was interrupted, the morning after you left here for Primrose, Harp's playful followers made a thorough house-to-house search of the town. Whatever items of food they found, they carted off with them to the saloon. I doubt though that they found very much till they came in here. That's what happened to Hoskins' stock. They took it."

"And left you nothing, huh?"

"Fortunately, they searched the cellar first, and what they found there apparently satisfied them because they didn't bother to look in the kitchen and see what I had in the cupboard. That's what we've been living on. And there isn't very much left of that either. Just about enough for tomorrow and that's all."

"Now I wish I hadda brought back everything instead of taking only a tiny part and dumpin' the rest. But getting back to Harp and his crew, the stuff they took from you couldn't have lasted very long. Not with all those mouths to be fed."

"No-o, I suppose not. You said you have coffee in that sack, didn't you?"

"About fifty pounds of it. Why?"

"I could go some right now. How about you?"

"Sounds good to me too."

"Only take a few minutes to boil the water for it. Want me to help you with that thing?"

"No. I can manage it all right."

Canavan bent over, got a grip on the sack and hoisted it to his shoulder.

"Feels like it weighs a ton now," he said, and shifted his burden a little. "All right. Let's go." He followed Daws upstairs. Minutes later, when he was straddling a kitchen chair and Daws was boiling the water for their coffee, Canavan said as he took off his hat and looked at it: "This one belongs to Voss. Had plenty of time to get another one when I was in Primrose, only I never gave it a thought." He put the hat in the chair next to his. "Oh, how's Ardis makin' out?" Daws turned his head and gave him a frowning look.

"Oh, yeah?" Canavan said, interpreting the look. "Been giving you a hard time, huh?"

"Well, as I predicted and I'm sure you must remember it just as I do, once she learned that I was going to furnish the food she was going to eat, that did it."

"How do you mean, that did it?"

"She invited herself to live here," Daws explained. "Closer to the source of supply, I guess. Oh, she's quite a young woman, Canavan. All you said she was and then some. In fact, a great deal more."

"Got her own way of figuring things out, hasn't she?"

"Indeed she has! The way she arrives at some conclusions, we-ll, just about leaves me speechless, stumped for words. And that's really something for a man to whom words have been his very life."

"Was she satisfied with what you told her about me having to go off to see somebody?" Canavan asked.

"She wasn't at all satisfied. And I don't think she believed me."

"And I still don't believe him," a voice that was Ardis Lundy's said from a doorway that led to a hallway and the rooms that opened upon it. Ardis, with an old, faded, almost threadbare robe gathered tightly around her, holding it closed over her bosom with one hand, and guarding the sash around her waist with the other, clutching the huge knot as though she was afraid it might burst open, looked hard at Canavan, then at Daws. She said to the latter: "Yes, this is yours, Mr. Daws. I found it hanging in the closet in my room and I took the liberty of putting it on. It doesn't smell very good though. Rather musty. It probably hasn't been hung out to air for a long time, and goodness knows everything needs airing out every now and then. As for you, Canavan," and again her eyes held on him, "I'm disappointed in you."

"You don't say! And what brought that about, as though I don't know?"

"I think you should have let me know you were going off somewhere instead of making it necessary for me to find it out from someone else," she said evenly.

"Since when do I have to account to you for what I do?"

"Aren't you forgetting something?"

"Oh, we gonna go through that again? For the last time, Ardis, and you'd better believe it this time, I'm no more responsible for you, for what you do, or for what happens to you than –"

"Go some coffee, Mrs. Lundy?" Daws asked, plainly embarrassed by the sharpening tone in Canavan's voice, and apparently anxious to avoid a scene between Canavan and the young widow.

"Yes, thank you, Mr. Daws," Ardis said.

She advanced into the room, came up to the table, drew out a chair and seated herself opposite Canavan, and met his eyes unflinchingly.

"Might as well tell you this too," Canavan went on. "Soon as things get back to the way they were around here, I'll be pulling out of Paradise and heading for California."

"You can go anywhere you like."

"Well, now, thanks. That's mighty big of you."

"As long as you provide for me before you go," Ardis added with exasperating calm.

Canavan smiled back at her, his smile covering up the burning in his eyes.

"I don't aim to do anything for you or about you," he said with deliberate, matching calm. "Now what do you think of that?" He reached for his hat, caught it up and clapped it on his head, and got up on his feet. "Never mind pourin' any coffee for me, Daws. I haven't any taste for it now."

He swung his chair around and shoved it in close to the table, turned and walked doorward.

"I'll bet it was a woman you went to see," Ardis called after him.

He stopped and looked back at her and smiled fleetingly.

"How'd you guess? Can't fool you any, can I?"

"It was a woman, wasn't it?"

He didn't answer. Instead, he permitted his deliberately deepened smile to answer for him and went out of the room. As he came off the stairs, turned on the darkened street floor and headed for the back door, he stopped just long enough to call: "Hey, Daws! You'd better come down here and lock up after me!"

Canavan's return to the hotel began with a surprise and ended with one. First, gliding up to the back door, he was agreeably surprised to find that it was unlocked. He opened it quietly, slipped inside and closed it again. As he emerged into the tiny lobby he was surprised to find the ceiling light burning brightly. He was even more surprised when he saw Sam Voss behind the counter, idly turning the pages of a badly worn-looking book that Canavan judged was the register. Voss looked up when he felt Canavan's eyes on him, hastily waved him back out of sight, came out from behind the counter and led him through a curtained doorway into a small room off the lobby. Canavan eyed him wonderingly.

"What's the matter?" he asked in a guarded voice.

"Got the place crawlin' with cattlemen," Voss whispered back to him.

Canavan's eyebrows arched.

"Had to give them your room too. You won't mind sleeping down here, will you?"

"No, 'course not, Voss. One place is as good as another. But how come the cattlemen are here? Something up?"

"And how there is!" Voss replied. "The cattlemen came into town because the judge sent for them. Said he had something important to discuss with them. I overheard some of them jawin' away upstairs. That's how I know what's doing."

"Go on," Canavan urged him. "I'm listening."

Voss poked his head out, stole a quick look outside; apparently there was no one in the lobby for he withdrew his head.

"I haven't any use for Harp. Chances are a helluva lot less than anybody else in this town. But I'll say one thing for him," Voss continued. "When he's got something on his mind, he doesn't beat around. He comes right out with it. Speaks his piece and stands by it. When he had the ranchers together in that back room of his, he laid it right smack on the line for them. Told them he's willing to go along with them same as always, backing them against nesters and everybody else. But being that he's lost his income on account of the storekeepers closing up on him and doing him out of what he was makin' them pony up every week, he thinks the cattlemen ought to make up to him what he's losing."

Canavan shook his head and commented: "Got his nerve with him, all right."

"Wouldn't be where he is now if he didn't have it," the hotel-keeper responded. "Anyway, by the time he got finished speakin' his piece, it was late, and with so many of the cattlemen having such a long way to go to get home, they decided to stay over for the night. That way they've got a chance to get together without the judge and talk things over among themselves."

"Oh, then they haven't given Harp their answer yet."

"Nope. Not yet they haven't."

"Got any idea from what you overheard how they feel about this thing?" Canavan asked.

Voss nodded. "They don't like it," he said simply.

"That's good."

"Y'see," Voss went on, "most of them aren't doing so good. Just about breaking even. Maybe if they were makin' dough, it might be different. Maybe then they wouldn't put up such a holler about having to kick in to the judge. But with things the way they are, they don't like the idea. What's happened, they say, is Harp's fault, every last bit of it too, and they don't see why they should have to make good for his mistakes. Almost all of them that I heard squawkin' said Harp was 'way out of line with the storekeepers. The way he laid it in to them, making them pay more and more all the time for the privilege of doing business in Paradise, we-ll, it figured the time would come when they wouldn't be able to keep meeting his demands and still make a profit for themselves. That time's finally come. So with Harp to blame for it, the cattlemen want him to figure his own way out of the mess he's made for himself. But they don't want him to do it at their expense."

"I've been wondering if it came to a showdown between Harp and them – and it figured it would have to come sooner or later –"

"Yeah?"

"– if they'd have the guts to buck him."

"You don't have to wonder any longer, Mister," Voss answered. "Because I can tell you."

"You think they'll fight if he crowds them?"

"They sure will. All the way down the line too, and to the last man. I know the cattlemen, Mister. I've known them for a long, long time, too. So I oughta know what I'm talking about. And when I tell you they won't kowtow and knuckle down to the judge, you can take my word for it they won't."

"Then the way you see it, Harp's bitten off a helluva bigger bite than he can chew."

"That's right. But even so, him realizing that, I mean, he can't afford to back down now. He's got to stick to what he says he wants."

"And if the cattlemen turn him down as you think they will . . . ?"

"Then there'll be hell to pay," Voss said simply. "Harp will try to force them to kick in, and they'll fight. There'll be gunplay and killings, and where it will end will depend on just two things. Men and guns, and on whichever side can do the most with the men and guns it has."

"Who usually does the talking for the cattlemen?"

"That'd be Milo Sturdevant."

"Tell me about him."

"Milo's far and away the richest man in the county. Runs the biggest and best-payin' spread and saddles the biggest crew. He's an old blood-and-guts man. A real firebrand."

"He upstairs now too?"

"Yeah, sure," Voss said, nodding. "But why d'you ask? You got something in mind?"

"I might have."

"I'd think twice if I was you, Mister, before I tackled old Milo and the others. You'll probably find they've got it in for you, and good."

"Why? What did I ever do to them?"

"You're forgetting about that Lundy feller, aren't you?"

"What about him?"

"Aw, come on now! You know what I mean."

"I will when you tell me," Canavan insisted.

"Mister, maybe you don't know it, but everybody knows it was you who helped Lundy bust out of the sheriff's office the night before he was supposed to be hanged. And since it was the cattlemen who had him brought in and sentenced to be hanged for killing a cattleman, only to have you step in and save him from the rope –"

"But he's dead," Canavan said, interrupting him.

"I know. But I don't know how they feel about it, whether they're satisfied or not. Anyway, what I'm trying to tell you is that I don't think they'd cotton to the idea of having you try to tell them what to do."

"How'd you know I had anything to do with freeing Lundy? Who'd you get it from?"

"First from one of the storekeepers who happened to be in the saloon and who heard Harp's crew talking about it and about what they were gonna do to you for butting into something that wasn't any of your business."

"H'm," Canavan said. "And then?"

"Then I heard it from somebody else too."

"That somebody else couldn't have been Mrs. Lundy, could it?"

"Well, now, I don't exactly remember."

"It doesn't matter any more. So forget it. Where'll I find this fire-spouting Milo Sturdevant?"

"Hope you're doing the right thing by yourself going up to see him."

"That's something I won't know for sure till after I've seen him."

Sam Voss' shoulders lifted in a futile shrug.

"All right," he said. "All I could do was tell you what I thought, and I've done that. Now it's up to you. You oughta know what you're doing and what you're liable to be letting yourself in for. Room Ten, Mister. That's the big double room down the end of the hall. I put Sturdevant and John Gasson in there. They're neighbors and seem to get along together, even though they're about as different from each other as they can be, with Milo always hollering about something or other and John so blamed stingy with words you'd think they cost him something. You'll probably find all the others in there with them, and more'n likely, they'll all be talking at the same time. Anyway, good luck. Hope you make out all right."

Every door along the dimly lighted landing, even the one to the room which he had occupied, was open, and Canavan, striding by, got a fleeting glimpse inside the rooms. There was no one in any of them. But all showed signs of occupancy. There were hats tossed on some of the beds; others were a little rumpled and a little hollowed – indications that they had been sat on. Then as he neared the far end of the landing he heard a hum of voices just beyond him. Thin clouds of tobacco smoke drifted out from the last room, climbed lazily and finally wavered to a stop a foot or so below the landing ceiling, and hung motionlessly in the air. Then, apparently his step was heard by someone in the room for he heard a voice say, "Sh-h! Hold it a minute, you fellers. Think somebody's coming down the hall." The hum of voices died out. Canavan came up to the doorway and stopped. More tobacco smoke drifted out, floated past him and climbed upward. A pall of smoke hung over the room itself, with at least half of the men present contributing to it. There were two beds in the room, one on each side of the door, and directly opposite the door was a window. A couple of men were perched on each of the beds, two others were seated on the window sill, another leaned against the bureau, and five others stood around the room, some of them backed against the walls and standing a little spread-legged.

A man came forward, a tall, lean, graying man with thin, tight lips, bright, hard eyes, and a rather thin and pointed nose framed in a bronzed, lined face. He looked at Canavan questioningly.

"Yeah?" he asked a bit curtly.

"I'm looking for Milo Sturdevant," Canavan told him.

"I'm Sturdevant. Who are you, and what d'you want?"

"Like to talk to you for a minute."

"All right," Sturdevant said and he gestured. "Talk."

"Hold it, Milo," a man who was sitting on one of the beds said. He got up on his feet and came forward to Sturdevant's side and peered hard at Canavan. "Thought I recognized you, Mister. Took another look though to make sure. You're Canavan, aren't you?"

"That's right," Canavan acknowledged.

"Canavan?" Sturdevant repeated.

"Yeah. The feller who helped that goddamned Lundy bust out of Jerry Turner's place the night before we were gonna string him up."

"You don't say!" came from Sturdevant.

"Hey, ain't he the one who jumped the Russell boy down at the lunchroom and killed him?" another man, a standee, asked.

"I killed him when Vasco and he tried to brace me," Canavan said quietly.

"That's your story, Mister, and not the way we heard it," Sturdevant retorted. "I kinda think we owe you something and that we oughta square up with you."

Clumsily, his body half-turning, the cattleman went for his gun. But he did not complete the draw; his hand stopped in midair, inches from the butt of his hip-worn gun when he suddenly found Canavan's gun yawning at him. He stared unbelievingly, blinked and stared hard again.

"I didn't come up here for this," Canavan said evenly. "But if this is the way you want it, it'll be all right with me."

Sturdevant glowered at him and slowly

brought up his right hand, away from his gun, and Canavan grunted and holstered his own gun.

"I came up here to tell you something," he said quietly, "and I think you'd better listen. 'Course what you do after I've had my say is up to you. I'm just hoping you're smart enough to take a tip when it's offered."

Sturdevant backed off a step or two, turned and stalked away, stopped and stood next to the man who was leaning against the bureau, and continued to glare at Canavan. The latter sauntered inside, closed the door behind him with a backward thrust of his leg, backed against the closed door and eased his hat up from his forehead. Shuttling his gaze around the room from man to man to complete taking in the full circle of faces that were turned to him, he said simply: "I know why you men are here."

Unconsciously he hooked his thumbs in his belt. He pretended not to notice the eyes that left his face with the movement of his hands and coursed downward and held on his thigh-worn, tied-down gun. He could read the cattlemen's thoughts, they were so plainly written in their faces. In a land where it was the custom for every man to wear a gun, those, like the cattlemen, who wore difficult-to-reach hip-riding guns and who seldom attained any marked proficiency with them, had a wholesome respect for a low-slung gun. It was the mark of a man who was skilled in its handling, and it was a warning to those whom he encountered not to go out of their way to antagonize such a man, for the slightest provocation might bring it flashing from its cut-away holster spewing lead and dealing out death. Canavan sensed the effect his gun was having on the cattlemen, and he took full advantage of it. He knew he could speak plainly and openly, and even if his listeners disagreed with him, they wouldn't be likely to interrupt him. Even the glowering Sturdevant would think twice before he ventured to voice a dissenting opinion.

"I said I know why you men are here," Canavan began again. "I'm hoping for your sake and for Paradise's too, that you don't give in to Harp. He's coming to the end of his rope and whoever sides in with him will go down with him. You've got a chance to break with him. Take advantage of it. There'll be a marshal in Paradise one of these days, and once he starts pokin' his nose into things, there'll be trouble. Real trouble, too. Now I want to give you men this one piece of advice. Some of you, I know, won't take it. But you others, you men who can see further than the ends of your noses, think about it, and think about it hard. There isn't a one of you here who is clean. You've all got blood on your hands. Nester blood. But you can make it easier on yourselves for that day of reckoning that's sure to come, and maybe a heap sooner than you think, if you tell Harp it's no deal, and if you stick to it, and let him go down by himself."

He paused, ranged his eyes again around the room. The gazes of the men on every side of him had come up again and were fixed on him.

"Now there's just this much more," he went on. "The law they passed in Washington last year gives nesters the right to file and settle on the land that hasn't been filed on already. That holds good here and everywhere else in the west. I know, I know. You've all put time and work and some of you have put money into land that you've been using for grazing your stock. But you never filed on that land. And now that you know you're going to lose it, if you haven't lost it already, you think you're going to beat the law by killing off every nester who shows up here. If that's what you think, you couldn't be more wrong. You aren't bucking local law. You're bucking the gover'ment, the United

States gover'ment, and you aren't big enough or strong enough to do that and get away with it. The first thing you know you'll find you've bitten off a helluva bigger piece than you can chew. But by then it'll be too late. You'll be in for it. That's it. That's what I came up here to say. What you do about it is up to you. But one thing you can bet on. Go on the way you've been doing, flaunting the law like you were bigger than it, riding roughshod over the nesters like they were dirt under your feet, and so on, and see what happens to you."

He reached behind him for the doorknob, opened the door and went out. But he purposely did not close it after him. He knew there would be an immediate and doubtless violent exception to what he had said, with Milo Sturdevant's angry voice rising above the others, and he hoped to be able to hear some of it. He slowed his step and listened hopefully.

"You wanna know something, Milo?" he heard as he neared the stairway and he slowed his step even more. "That marshal he was talking about..."

"Well?" the voice was impatient, sharp and curt, and Canavan knew it had to be Sturdevant's. "What about him?"

"I think he was talking about himself. I think he's a lawman."

Canavan halted, and half-turned, listened even more attentively.

"G'wan!" Sturdevant retorted and there was scorn in his voice. "He's no lawman any more than . . . you are!"

"And I still think he is."

"I'll tell you what he is," Sturdevant went on. "I think he's the kind who hasn't anything better to do with himself 'cept go 'round stickin' his nose into other folks' business. Now what d'you think of that?"

"It's a free country, Milo."

"Sure, and you can think anything you like. Only remember what I said and see if I'm not right about him. And the next time you run into him, you can tell him this for me. Tell him to butt out of our business. If he doesn't —"

"He doesn't look like the kind you can tell anything like that to."

"Oh, got you buffaloed, huh? Well, he doesn't scare me any. So I'll tell it to him myself." Then Sturdevant's voice flared. "And somebody close that goddamned door before some other flannel-mouth comes bargin' in on us and tries to tell us what to do!"

Canavan heard the door slam as he started down the stairs.

The next morning Sam Voss shook the sleeping Canavan into awakening.

" 'Smatter?" the latter wanted to know, peering up at the hotel-keeper through heavy-lidded eyes and brushing his mussed hair back from them.

"Sh-h," Voss cautioned him. "Keep your voice down. Something's up. I went outside like I do every morning to sweep down the walk, and a couple of the judge's gunslicks were out front and they chased me back inside, said nobody's allowed out of the hotel until Harp gets here. Then I just took a look out the back way and Harp's got a couple more of his hands posted out there. Better get up and into your clothes."

"Yeah, sure," Canavan, fully awake by then, told him. "Where'll you be?"

"Sweepin' down upstairs. But you stay put. I'll let you know what happens."

"What about them upstairs?" Canavan asked, kicking off the covers and swinging his long, drawer-clad legs and bare feet over the side of the cot. "You wake them already and tell them something's up?"

"I'm on my way upstairs right now," Voss answered and left him.

It took Canavan but a couple of minutes to get dressed. On tiptoe he sidled up to the door that opened into the lobby, put his ear against it and listened. He couldn't hear anything and decided that Harp hadn't arrived yet.

"Wonder what the old buzzard is up to?" he asked himself. But there was no ready explanation that he could advance. "But I'm still willing to bet he's up to something, and knowing the way he operates, it can't be anything good."

He stepped back from the door, turned and went to the kitchen, and lifting a corner of the fully drawn window blind the barest bit, stole a cautious look outside. A man was standing back-turned just beyond the back door. Canavan moved so that he might get a wider view of the back yard and promptly spotted two more men standing together a little beyond the hotel and looking up at it. He eased down the blind and retraced his steps to the door off the lobby and listened there again. There were heavy bootsteps, movement that reflected the entrance of several men, and he heard a thick voice call: "Hey, Voss! Get the cattlemen down here! The judge has something to say to them!"

"Here it comes," Canavan murmured. "Won't have to wonder any longer."

There was a brief wait. Canavan, with his ear glued to the door, could hear movement outside of it, creaking floorboards under booted feet in a back-and-forth sauntering-about. It stopped, rather abruptly he thought, and before he could begin to wonder why, a voice that he recognized at once as Harp's said: "Ah. Good morning, gentlemen. I trust you slept well." Canavan listened for it but he did not hear any response from the cattlemen who he assumed were bunched together on the stairway. "Have you arrived at a decision yet?"

"Not yet, Judge," a voice that Canavan knew was Milo Sturdevant's answered. "We've done a heap of talking, but that's about as far as we've got up to now. But there isn't any rush, is there?"

"Oh, but there is indeed, Sturdevant," Harp said quickly. "I thought you and your associates understood that."

"No-o, can't say we did, Judge. You said you wanted to know as soon as possible, but you didn't say anything about having to know right away."

"That's unfortunate because conditions and circumstances have changed considerably since we had our little talk. Hence it is imperative that I have an immediate answer."

"He must know something's happened to the wagon," Canavan decided, "and that he isn't gonna get anything from Primrose this trip. Maybe now he's worried and figures he's gotta make a fast move of some kind, or be prepared to make one, and that he'd better have dough. That's probably why he's putting on the pressure. After I turned the horses loose and dumped the wagon, I should've run them back to Primrose instead of letting them head back here. They must've got back and that's how he knows."

"I'm afraid you're gonna have to wait till we have one for you, Judge," Canavan heard Sturdevant reply.

"Unfortunately, I can't wait," Harp said, "and since you people have already taken too much time and without fruitful result, I think I'd better help you make up your minds. Not directly because I wouldn't want to influence you. But indirectly." He paused for a moment, and then he went on again. "Now as you know, there isn't any food in town. And since we have a very limited supply, just about enough for ourselves, we cannot, and I regret that deeply, undertake to feed you men too. Then too, and I am genuinely sorry to have to do this, no one will be permitted to leave these premises till you have arrived at a decision."

"Why, the scurvy son-uva-gun," Canavan muttered darkly to himself. "He's genuinely sorry, all right, but he isn't gonna let that keep him from starving them into doing what he wants."

"Oh, just a word of caution, gentlemen," he heard Harp say. "So you won't do anything hasty or rash. My men have been posted at both the front and back doors to this building. Neither they nor I have any desire to inflict bodily harm upon any of our friends. So please don't force us to. When you have an answer for me, Sturdevant, signal one of my men at the front door and he will be glad to summon me. That's all, gentlemen."

IX

It was some minutes after Harp had gone, and his men had withdrawn to the street with a window-rattling slam of the front door that Sam Voss came scurrying back to the little room off the lobby. Canavan, sitting hunched over on the edge of his cot, raised his eyes to him, took note of the flush that was riding in Voss' cheeks and recognized the exciting effect the judge's staggering announcement had had upon the usually pallid-faced hotel-keeper.

"I wish you coulda heard him," Voss

practically burst out with. His flat chest heaved a little. "For downright, honest-to-God gall, that Harp maverick just about beats everybody else I've ever run up against and I've had dealings with some of the damnedest, nerviest characters you could ever hope to –"

"I heard him."

"Oh," Voss said, and his tone and expression reflected his disappointment and made Canavan sorry he hadn't held his tongue. "What do you think?"

Canavan's rounded shoulders lifted. "What's there to think?"

"Well, what d'you think is gonna happen?" Voss pressed him.

"Only one of two things, Voss," Canavan replied. "The cattlemen will kick in as Harp wants them to, or they won't. It's that simple. I'll admit though they haven't much choice, not the way he's got them bottled up in here. So they'll probably have to give in to him and that'll be that."

"Yeah, but supposing they don't? What d'you think he'll do then?"

"I don't think he'll do anything 'cept keep trying, and if one scheme doesn't work, then he'll try another. They've got the money he needs, and he's got to get it. But I don't think he'll lose his head and do anything to them to get it. He can't afford to do that.

Suppose they should decide to take a chance on a break-out and a shoot-out with Harp's gun-throwers? That would be the worst thing that could happen to Harp. You can't get anything out of a dead man, and depend on it, Voss, Harp knows that. So I kinda think he hopes to cow them into staying put, starve them, and when their empty bellies start growling back at them, that they'll give in and agree to what he wants. The cattlemen know I'm still around?"

"Dunno. Haven't heard any of them mention your name. But why'd you ask? Oh, you got an idea or something on how to beat Harp kickin' around up there?" Voss asked, pointing with a broken-nailed finger to Canavan's head.

"Y'think Sturdevant would come down here for a minute?"

"Mean you wanna talk to him?"

"That's the general idea," Canavan said dryly.

"I suppose I can ask him if you want me to."

"D'you mind?"

"All he can say is 'No.'"

"That's right. How about asking him now?"

Voss thought about it for a moment as Canavan watched him, studying him, then he said: "All right. I'll go ask him now," and went out.

Again there was a brief wait. But then, just as Canavan got up on his feet, Voss returned, and with him, trooping in at his heels, came a frowning Sturdevant.

"Well?" he demanded of Canavan. "What d'you want?"

"Looks to me like Harp's got you fellers where the hair is short, or don't you think so?"

"Either way, what's it got to do with you?"

Canavan smiled.

"You're gonna give in to him, aren't you, and kick in the way he wants?" Sturdevant didn't answer. "Guess he knows you're scared to death of him and that he can push you around all he likes. He must, or he wouldn't manhandle you the way he's doing. Helluva thing to see a full-grown man who's supposed to be a leader so scared of another man. And you are, aren't you?"

Sturdevant glowered at Canavan and wheeled around to the door and Canavan laughed.

"That's it," he taunted. "Run. That's what I expected you to do. You're all mouth, Sturdevant. You haven't got the guts of a louse. That's the way I had you pegged right from the start and now you're proving how right I was. Go 'head. G'wan back upstairs to your side-partners and talk some more. Big and loud too. And after you get done talking, you can get down on your belly, you and the others, and go crawling to Harp and beg him to take your money. Because that's what you're gonna do, isn't it? Or what it amounts to?"

Sturdevant, with his bony hand curled around the door-knob, stiffened. Slowly, straightening up to his full height, he turned around again. His eyes were burning. Little patches of crimson were dancing in his tanned cheeks.

"Voss said you had some idea you thought we might be able to use to beat Harp," he said evenly, fighting down his fury.

Canavan looked hard, wide-eyed, at him.

"Huh? Y'mean you're not gonna knuckle down to him? Y'mean you're gonna fight back?"

Again the goaded cattleman managed to control himself.

"This idea of yours . . ."

Canavan repeated what he had said to Voss. Sturdevant listened attentively and made no attempt to interrupt him.

"Now my idea is for you fellers to play along with Harp. Let him think you're gonna hold out. I think he expects you to do that, leastways for a while, till you're so starved out that you'll be willing to agree to anything. Like I said, I think he expects you to do that, and to make it look good, I don't think you oughta do anything to disappoint him. But meanwhile, while you fellers are playing your little game with him, I can be out rounding up your crew and the other cattlemen's outfits, and the minute we're set, come sweeping down on Paradise and hit it from all sides."

Sturdevant said "H'm," but that was all.

"Now once Harp sees what he's in for, I expect him to pull out of the saloon with his gang of gunnies and fight his way up the street and make his stand here. Think about it, Sturdevant, and see if it doesn't make sense. And try to figure the way Harp will. If he can get in here, he'll be over the hump. He'll have you fellers to use against us. He'll offer to trade with us, his life and our promise to let him go in exchange for your lives. That's if he sees things are going against him. And we won't be able to turn him down. But there's one way we can kinda put a crimp in his plans. It'll mean that you cattlemen will have to fight. You'll have to stop him from getting upstairs. If you can keep him pinned down in the lobby while we're closing in on him from the outside, we'll squeeze the guts out of him. And that'll mean the end of him and his crew. Now what d'you think?"

Sturdevant didn't answer right away; thoughtfully, he rubbed his chin with the back of his hand, then he lifted his eyes to meet Canavan's, nodded and said: "Sounds all right, and with any luck at all, we oughta be able to pull it off. But how d'you plan to break out of here with Harp's gun-slicks surrounding the place?"

"I don't aim to try and shoot my way out," Canavan said dryly.

"Didn't think you did," the cattleman retorted. "Not if you've got any sense."

"Suppose you leave it to me to work out?"

"All right," Sturdevant answered. "You figure out that part for yourself. Now there's just one thing that I'd like you to tell me."

"What's that?"

"And I want a straight-out answer."

"That's the only kind you'll get from me."

"I don't get you, Canavan. No man in his right mind lays his life on the line for a lot o' strangers who don't mean anything to him. 'Less of course he's angling for something that he figures is worth the risk he's running. Now what are you after? What do you expect to get out of this? And don't try to tell me you aren't looking for something because I won't believe you."

"I won't try to tell you anything, Sturdevant," Canavan replied. "Aside from knowing damned well, and even without you telling me, that you wouldn't believe me, I don't think you'd understand."

"H'm," the cattleman said again.

"I'm offering you a way to beat Harp and get rid of him. Now it's up to you. Take it or leave it."

Voss, who had been standing by silently, simply looking from one to the other, coughed behind his hand, and when Sturdevant glanced at him mechanically, Voss said: "With just about everybody in town knowing that it was Canavan who helped that nester Lundy break out of the sheriff's place, I figure you must know it too. Now nobody asked Canavan to do it. Nobody even knew him, being that he'd just hit town. But he risked his own neck because he wanted to help Lundy. Maybe because the way he'd heard it, he didn't think Lundy had had a fair and square trial, and he, Canavan, felt Lundy should've. Anyway, whatever reason he might've had for doing it, he did it, and the fact that Lundy didn't get away when he had the chance, we-ll, that wasn't Canavan's fault. It was Lundy's. And never mind askin' me how I know that.

It isn't important. What is important though is this, the point I'm trying to make. Y'know, Milo, just because you can't understand what makes a man do things he doesn't have to do, don't you go on thinking –"

Sturdevant stopped him with a frown and an upraised, spread-fingered hand, and turned away from him.

"When do you figure to make your break?" he asked Canavan.

"Tonight," the latter answered, and added: "When it's good and dark. Probably around midnight."

"Anything we can do to help?"

Canavan shook his head.

"Anything you want or think you might need?"

"Just your foreman's name and the shortest way to your place."

"Want me to tell you now, or before you go?"

"When I'm ready to go will be time enough."

"You know where I'll be when you want me."

"Yeah, sure."

Sturdevant nodded, turned and opened the door, looked back over his shoulder at Canavan for a long moment, and finally said: "Wanna tell you something, Canavan.

When I came out here, I had this," he patted his holstered gun, "a rifle in my saddleboot, a kinda thin-worn blanket and my horse. I didn't have enough dough in my kick to buy me a cup o' coffee even if there'd've been a place where they sold it. I met up with a wagon train headin' west and I traded off the rifle and the saddle for a sack o' grub, some tools and seven bucks, all the dough the train leader had. I built me a shack to live in and rigged up a lean-to for my horse, then I went to work stakin' out my spread and clearing the land. I went through just about everything you've ever heard tell of, from sickness to fire, from dry spells to storms and floods. I stood off Indians and whites who were even worse than the Indians. I know what it's like to be so beat that I couldn't even pull off my boots. I know what it's like to be lonely too. If you don't think it took guts to come through all the hell I've known, and still have enough left to make myself go on, you've got another think coming. So, Mister, don't you ever talk to me again the way you did. I'm old now, and I know I'm not as fast on the draw as I used to be. But that won't stop me from climbin' all over you the next time and makin' you eat your words. You remember that and we'll get along. We mightn't agree on things, but we'll still get along."

Canavan was willing to admit he was asking a lot when he hoped the night would be dark, so dark in fact that he wouldn't be able to see his hand in front of his face. At midnight, when he climbed the ladder that led to the hotel roof, he wasn't overly optimistic. But when he peered out over the rim of the uncovered skylight and found there was no moon that night, no stars either, and a limitless black canopy for a sky, he was grateful. He withdrew his head, shifted himself around on the ladder rung and peered down at Sam Voss who was looking up at him from the landing.

"How is it?" the hotel-keeper asked in a guarded voice.

"Made to order for me," Canavan hissed back at him. "Black as pitch. Now how about that plank? Wanna start passing it up to me?"

If Voss answered, Canavan failed to hear him. He was about to repeat his question when the sound of something being moved carried upward to him, and he checked himself and waited. A long, thick plank that Voss and he had brought upstairs from the cellar earlier that evening and which Canavan had propped up against the landing wall within arm's reach of the ladder, began to nose upward. When he heard it thump, then scrape against the ladder, he hastily stepped off onto the roof. Hunching over and gripping the end of the plank as it emerged from the skylight, he began to back off with it. When it was clear of the skylight, he bent over, curled one arm around the plank and half carried, half dragged it to the side of the roof and cautiously peered down over the edge. At first he couldn't see anything; the darkness was too thick and too blanketing. But a longer, more lingering and more intense look finally penetrated the darkness, and he was able to make out the shadowy figure of a man idling at the very bottom of the alley slope with the back yard about a step beyond him. Now Canavan was confronted by a serious problem, how to draw the man away from there. He was frowning over it when the man himself provided the solution; he suddenly sauntered away and disappeared from view. Canavan moved alertly to take advantage of his unexpected good fortune.

The plank was some eighteen feet long, and the alley, according to Voss, exactly fifteen feet in width. Kneeling and pushing out the plank, Canavan managed to bridge the alley with it, heard it thump when it touched down on the adjoining building's roof. Pushing it outward even more, he heard it scrape as it tore away some of the roof's tarred surface.

When he was satisfied that it was resting quite securely on both roofs, he raised up a little and stole another quick and anxious look below. His probing eyes failed to uncover any sign of the man who had walked off from there.

"Probably chewin' the fat with another one of Harp's hands somewhere 'round the back," he muttered to himself. "Hope he's the long-winded kind and likes to talk. If he'll just give me enough time to get across and haul in the plank so he won't be able to see it if he comes strolling back and happens to look up . . ."

He mounted the plank on his hands and knees and crawled across it without incident, and got off it on the adjoining roof. Swiftly he drew in the plank, hoisted it to his shoulder and carried it away to the far side and, repeating the performance, spanned the second alley. By the time he had bridged the fourth alley, he was wheezing and chest-heaving from his exertions. Despite the fact that all of the buildings on the same side of the street with the hotel were of about the same height and his roof-top jaunt presented no problem now, he made slower progress the further upstreet he went. The plank was heavy, and carrying it took a toll of his arms and shoulders. When he came to the very last building, he breathed a deep sigh of relief for there he was able to abandon the plank. He unwound the coil of rope he had hung around his neck, slip-knotted and looped one end around a thick, firmly rooted iron pipe that he found poking some two feet skyward from the roof, backed off from it as he played out the rope, dropped the coil over the side and, easing himself over the edge, let himself down to the ground. His hands were sore, rope-burned and full of splinters from contact with the plank. But there was no time then to do anything to ease them. They would have to wait for a more leisurely time. Wryly he wondered when that would be.

Hugging the wall of the building, he followed it down the slanting length of the alley. As he neared the back yard, he heard the muffled stamp of a horse's pawing hoof and the animal's snort. Then as he rounded the building, a lean-to suddenly loomed up squarely in his path. He seemed a little surprised, and showed it by slowing his step, stopping altogether, and ranging a quick look about him. As he remembered it, the lean-to was located in the back yard, but farther back, he thought, from the alley. But there wasn't another one that he could see, so acknowledging that he must have mistaken its exact location, he hurried on to it, whipped back the tattered, half-torn-away canvas curtain that served as its door. In another minute he was backing Aggie out of it. She sought to nuzzle him, to show him how delighted she was to see him again. He had to push her off, and told her curtly, perhaps a little grumpily, too, because his roof-top-scaling and alley-spanning had taken something out of him: "Cut it, Aggie. We've got more important things to do."

She protested, mildly though. But she stopped her whinnying when he climbed up on her back. She wheeled away with him almost at once, before he had fully settled himself in the saddle. She took the upgrade just ahead of them in full, drumming stride, and paused quiveringly when she topped it. She wheeled again at his insistence, swung rather wide around the town below them, and when he whacked her with his hand, she snorted again and bounded away westward. They disappeared into the night and the enveloping darkness.

An arched gateway just off the road led to the Sturdevant place. A signboard bearing a legend that Canavan couldn't make out although he was sure it bore the name of the spread's quick-tempered owner, hung on short cuts of chain from the middle of the arch. When the night breeze, suddenly sweeping down, caught it, it swung back and forth; the board itself creaked a little, and the chain links rasped as they scraped against each other. Aggie pranced through the gateway and slowed her step to a mere walk when Canavan signaled. A tall, towering barn and what appeared to be a toolshed flanked the gateway on one side; on the other side was a low, squat building that Canavan at first glance promptly identified as the bunkhouse. A second and closer look revealed the fact that it was unusually long. However, that wasn't particularly surprising in view of what Sam Voss had told him about Sturdevant. It had to be a sizable structure, he told himself, to house a crew the size of Sturdevant's. His attention was attracted to the corral, just past the bunkhouse, when a sudden ray of light pierced the darkness, held for an instant on a post and ran along a short section of the top rail, highlighting its smooth-worn surface. Then the ray was gone again. He took it for granted the corral was sized in keeping with the number of horses that Sturdevant's riders might turn loose into it. Canavan's gaze lifted. Some fifty feet, or so he judged it to be, beyond the corral and facing the gateway squarely, was a hulking, shadow-draped building. Canavan wondered if Sturdevant had a family, or if he lived alone in the big house. Then coming abreast of the bunkhouse and halting Aggie in front of the door and turning in the saddle, he hollered: "Hey, Jolly! Nick Jolly!"

He was agreeably surprised and a little startled too when there was an immediate but somewhat begrudging and grumbly response from inside the darkened bunkhouse. "Yeah?"

"Got a message for you from your boss!" Canavan yelled, and he felt Aggie wince. She turned her head and looked up at him reproachfully.

There was a minute-long wait. Then the door was opened and flickering yellowish lantern-light flooded the doorway. The man who was holding the lantern came into view. Barefooted and clad in baggy, oversized long drawers and long-sleeved undershirt that was cuffed back at the wrists, he raised the lantern a bit higher and peered hard at Canavan who took note of a gun the man was clutching in his right hand. Aggie leveled a look at the man too.

"You Nick Jolly?" Canavan asked.

"Yeah. But who'n hell are you, and anybody ever tell you you've got the kind o' voice that could raise the dead? And how come my boss picked you to bring me a message?"

Canavan grinned and dismounted and sauntered up to the man.

"My name's Canavan," he began.

"Huh? Canavan?" Jolly repeated. He rubbed his chin with the back of his gun hand. "Wait a minute now. Think I've heard your name before. Aren't you the buzzard who helped that goddamned nester whatever his name was —"

"It was Lundy."

"That's right. The polecat we were gonna hang higher'n a kite for killing Vince Darrow. You helped him bust out of the sheriff's office the night before. Right?"

"Right," Canavan replied. "But I've been over that with your boss and long as he's satisfied, I don't think you should have anything to beef about."

"Oh, you don't, huh?" Jolly retorted heatedly. "Well, lemme tell you something, Canavan. Vince Darrow was —"

"I'm not interested in hearing anything about Vince Darrow," Canavan interrupted just as loudly. "He's dead. Besides I didn't know him. But from what I've heard tell about him, I think the less said about him, the better. That is, for him. Now get this, Jolly, and get it straight. I didn't come out here to have you tell me anything. I'm doing your boss and the other cattlemen a favor, a helluva big one too, and if you can't shut that big mouth of yours long enough to hear what I've got to say..."

He stopped because there was movement behind Jolly and two tousled and heavy-eyed men in about the same state of dress as Jolly appeared in the doorway.

" 'Smatter, Nick?" one of them asked.

"Yeah," the second man said. "Sounded like somebody was giving you a hard time, so we kinda thought we oughta come out and see what was goin' on. This feller –"

"G'wan back inside, you two," Jolly said curtly over his shoulder. "I can handle this and then some."

"Yeah, sure, Nick, only –"

"You heard me, didn't you?"

When Jolly turned his back on them, the two men who had been awakened from their sleep backed inside and padded away.

"Well?" Jolly demanded of Canavan. "You gonna tell me what Sturdevant had to say, or not?"

"If you think you can listen long enough."

"Look, Mister," Jolly began darkly.

Canavan's shoulders lifted. "I don't know if you know this," he began, "but Harp's been making the storekeepers in Paradise kick in to him every week. That's over with now. They've closed up and pulled out. So Harp's come up with the bright idea of having the cattlemen kick in to him to make up what he's losing as a result of it. He's putting the squeeze on Sturdevant and the others, Gasson, Hodges, Ruffing, and seven or eight others whose names I've forgotten."

"Go on," Jolly commanded.

"Harp's gunnies have got them holed up in Sam Voss' hotel and now nobody can get in or out. The idea is to keep them there without grub or anything and starve them into knuckling down to him and doing what he wants."

"Why, the son-uva-bitch!"

"I got hold of Sturdevant," Canavan continued, "and told him what I was gonna do. Break out of the place through the roof and using a plank get from building to building till I got to the end of the street where I'd left my horse. Then I said I'd head out this way first and get you fellers, then round up the men from the other spreads, and once we came together, we'd head for Paradise and hit it from all sides and put an end to Harp and his crew. Sturdevant gave me your name. That's how I happened to come hollering for you. That's the story, Jolly. What d'you wanna do about it?"

"You go back to your horse, Canavan, and climb up on him, and by the time you get yourself settled on him, you'll see the damnedest, fastest action you've ever seen."

"All right," Canavan answered, wheeled around and trudged back to the waiting mare. This time though, when Aggie sought to nuzzle him, he did not push her off; he accepted her show of affection and patted her in return and she whinnied happily. He vaulted up astride her.

Nick Jolly was no idle boaster. A moment after he stepped back inside the bunkhouse, the place came alive. Lights sputtered, steadied and flamed with a glary brightness that was reflected on the windowpanes. Excited voices could be heard from one end of the building to the other. There was a great deal of movement in the bunkhouse too, more of a scurrying-about than a normal, unhurried walking. Just as Canavan shifted himself, seeking a little more comfort in the saddle, the door was flung open and men began to stream out, some of them with their shirts unbuttoned and their pants in the process of being pulled up, others tucking in their shirttails. But all of them were booted and hatted and either wearing their guns or carrying them. With a quick look at Canavan and at the ground-pawing Aggie, they scurried away and ran off toward the barn. Lights suddenly blazed in there too and streamed out over the wooden ramp that led to it. Nick Jolly was the last to emerge from the bunkhouse. When he came out Canavan saw that he had armed himself with a rifle in addition to a hip-worn holstered gun.

Two mounted men rode out of the barn, clattered down the ramp and drummed across the shadowy ground to the bunkhouse and pulled up in front of Jolly.

"All right, you fellers," Canavan heard Jolly say to them. "We'll be waiting for you and the others a mile outside o' town. Don't keep us waiting too long though. Now get going and make those plugs earn their keep. Make them run!"

"Right, Nick!"

"Then get riding," Jolly added, gesturing them off.

The two horsemen backed their mounts, wheeled them and loped away.

"Wallop them good if they try to dog it on you!" Jolly yelled after them. Then, hitching up his pants, he came striding over to Canavan and looked up at him. "Well?" he asked. "We move fast enough to suit you?"

"Yeah, sure," Canavan replied. "How many men in your crew, Jolly?"

"Eighteen," was the answer. "Nineteen, counting me. And with the hands they oughta be able to round up from the other outfits we oughta come up with between thirty-five and forty."

"Uh-huh," Canavan said. "And about how many men d'you think Harp can throw against us?"

"Oh, about half as many, I'd say. Give or take one or two. Only there's one thing you wanna keep in mind. Most of Harp's hands are top gun-throwers, killers, and we aren't. So when one of Harp's gunnies throws a shot, chances are he'll hit with it. We'll probably miss with a couple and maybe hit with the third or fourth. So when you take that into consideration, you wanna figure that their twenty or so oughta be about equal to our, say, forty. But I can tell you this, Mister. My bunch won't dog it no matter what happens. They're good men, every last one o' them, and they'll fight. And Harp's killers will find that out damned quick once they tangle."

Hoofs thumped in swelling volume as mounted men rode out of the barn and down the ramp. A mounted man leading a saddled horse rode up to Jolly; the latter took the reins from him and climbed up on the riderless animal.

"All right, Canavan," he called briskly. "Let's go!"

Canavan wheeled away after him, overtook him almost at once, and rode alongside of him. The other horsemen, singly and by twos, fell in behind them and followed them out through the arched gateway, and wheeled onto the road when Jolly did. Loping after him and Canavan, they drummed townward.

"I suppose I shoulda left somebody behind to kinda keep an eye on things," Jolly said and Canavan turned to him. "But I know damned well that whoever I'da picked wouldn't have liked the idea. Soon's I told them what was going on in town and what the boss was up against, every last one of them hopped right up and made a grab for his clothes and his gun, and was all set to go. Funny, huh? 'Specially when you know Milo and how he can peel the hide off a man when he gets mad and starts lettin' him have a piece of his mind. And just about every man in the outfit, and that includes me, has had a taste of a Sturdevant tongue-lashing. But in spite of it, they all know the old man's fair and square, and they like him, and they're willing to fight for him. So the hell with it! If some thievin' maverick comes along and helps himself to something while we're away . . ."

He didn't finish. He simply lifted his rounded shoulders in a shrug. When his horse responded to Jolly's urging and lengthened his stride, Aggie voiced a high-pitched, nasal protest. Then not to be outdone, she suddenly bounded away. She was a couple of lengths ahead of Jolly's surprised horse in a matter of moments. Her scornful trumpeting that she flung back at him died abruptly, when Canavan pulled her to a stiff-legged, sliding halt and forced her to wait for the others to come up to them. She snorted angrily and tossed her head and fought to break away again. But Canavan's firm hand and the iron bit that cut into the corners of her mouth refused to compromise with her, and after a brief struggle she subsided and stood quietly. Then as a sign to Canavan that she was still angry with him, she began to grumble deep down in her throat. It sounded strangely enough like distant, muffled thunder. But Canavan paid no attention to it, and when Jolly and the other Sturdevant hands loped up, he pulled Aggie alongside of Jolly's horse and made her run along with him. The grumbling stopped shortly.

"What got into him?" Jolly asked.

"It's a her," Canavan told him.

"Well, him or her, what made the critter act up like that?"

"Guess she just felt like it."

"Which is why I never got married. No telling when a female's liable to burst out of the traces and kick hell out of whatever or whoever's near her."

Canavan offered no response. He had already noticed that there was no talking in the strung-out column. The deep darkness, he reasoned, the fact that most of the men were still wearied from their day's work, their sudden awakening, and the gravity of their mission, all combined, he told himself, to still their tongues.

"How much further we have to go?" he asked.

"Oh, we'll be there any minute now," Jolly replied.

They clattered past a heavily wooded section, and suddenly Jolly yelled: "Watch it now! We're turning off here!"

Despite his warning cry, horses trampled one another when those in front of them were pulled up sharply, and faltered and even stumbled and in some instances lost their footing when their riders, seeking to follow Jolly's lead, tried to wheel them up a grassy incline. There was some confusion, and here and there colliding men exchanged angry words. But once the first bunch of horses had safely negotiated the slope, and those behind them found the way open to them and proceeded to top it too, flaring tempers subsided.

"Well, now that we're here, we can wait," Jolly announced. "So take it easy, you fellers." Then in what was probably an attempt to relax them, he added wryly: "Some of you fellers who aren't so sure 'bout which end of the gun you're supposed to hold, now would be as good a time as any and maybe better than most for you to find out. So how about gettin' yourselves acquainted with those things you've all got swingin' from your hips?"

Someone laughed, and someone else, out of range of Canavan's hearing, muttered something that produced more laughter.

"That's a good sign," Jolly said low-voiced to Canavan. "When a man can laugh even when he knows there's more than just a passing chance that in a little while he's liable to get his fool head shot off, he'll be all right."

"Uh-huh," Canavan answered.

"That's why I said before they'll do all right for themselves when they square off against Harp's gunnies."

"Uh-huh," Canavan said a second time.

But he couldn't help but wonder if Jolly were merely reaffirming his confidence in his men, or if that was his way of reassuring himself.

Canavan looked around. But in the darkness the waiting horsemen were screened from his probing eyes and their shadow-veiled faces gave him no clue to what they were thinking. He wondered if any of them had ever drawn on another man, wondered, too, how many of them had ever had to shoot their way out of trouble? How would they react, he wondered, when they found themselves fighting it out with desperate, professional gun-throwers? Would they panic and break when they saw their mates shot down before their very eyes, or would they stand their ground and fight back all the more determinedly?

He found himself thinking of the first time that he had drawn on another man. He remembered it so clearly, it was as though it had just happened instead of ten years before. He was twenty-two then. Sauntering downstreet one day in his home town, he heard a sudden, startling blast of gunfire come from the direction of the sheriff's office. He remembered coming to an abrupt, heart-stopping halt, so rigidly rooted to the ground that movement seemed impossible. The sheriff was his brother, his favorite brother, too. But then he saw a man come bolting out of Dan's office and run upstreet. Canavan did not remember stepping down into the gutter. But all of a sudden he found himself there, waiting, and he recalled marveling at his sudden calm. When the fleeing man, a troublesome townsman named

Ed Spears, neared him and spotted him and recognized him, he skidded to a stop and, cursing, went for his gun. Canavan went for his and beat Spears to the draw. He had never forgotten the sight of Spears, sprawled on his face in the gutter with blood seeping out of his holed body.

"Mind telling me something, Canavan?" he heard a voice ask.

"Huh?" His head jerked around. "You say something, Jolly?"

"Yeah. I wanted to know if you'd mind telling me something."

"Like what?"

"Well, like what you figure to get out of this?"

"Your boss wanted to know the same thing."

"Oh, yeah? And what did you tell him?"

"That I didn't think he'd understand," Canavan answered, "and that he wouldn't believe me."

"Y'mean if you told him."

"That's right."

"But you didn't tell him."

"No."

"And you don't think I'd understand or believe you either. Right?"

"No, I don't think you would either, Jolly."

"But how do you know I wouldn't?" Jolly

argued. "How can you tell without tryin' me first?"

"All right. Suppose I should say I'll get a lot o' satisfaction out of seeing Harp and his crew put out of business?"

"We-ll, let's see now. You a lawman, Canavan?"

"Nope."

"And I know damned well you aren't a preacher. And just for satisfaction you're willing to risk getting a slug through your head?"

"I told you you wouldn't understand."

"I've been kickin' around for nearly fifty years, Canavan. I've run across all kinds of people. But I've never met up with anybody who was willing to risk his neck for anybody else 'less there was something worthwhile in it for him."

Canavan made no response.

"You took a chance gettin' strung up yourself, a chance you didn't have to take, and I know damned well there couldn't have been anything in it for you when you helped that nester get away," Jolly continued. "So maybe you're doing this for the same reason. The fact that I don't understand it doesn't mean I don't believe you. Fact is, I do. Now don't go askin' me to tell you why. I wouldn't know what to say. But I know it takes all kinds of people to make up a world, and if you're the kind..."

The pounding beat of approaching horses' hoofs carried in the hushed night air, and reached them. Jolly promptly backed his horse away from Aggie.

"Here they come!" he hollered. "Let's go!"

Canavan followed him down the slope. The other men moved after them, and with them, lined the shoulder of the road. A strung-out band of shadowy horsemen galloped up; when Jolly yelled to them and rode out to meet them, they pulled their mounts to a sliding stop.

X

The wall clock in Sam Voss' kitchen boomed suddenly and woke the hotel-keeper who was dozing in his chair at the table. His bowed, bobbing head jerked downward. He opened his eyes, grimaced and rubbed the back of his neck, stopped and looked up at the clock. He scratched his head, rubbed his nose vigorously with the back of his hand, pushed back from the table and climbed stiffly to his feet. He trudged out to the lobby, stood beneath the ceiling light for a moment and just when it appeared that he was going to reach up and lower the light, he walked away. He halted at the foot of the stairs and listened. He could hear a low murmur of voices on the upper floor. He wasn't surprised though despite the lateness of the hour; no one, he knew, would sleep that night. The street door opened suddenly, startling him, and his head jerked around. Four of Harp's men came in, then Harp himself entered and closed the door behind him. His men separated and each sauntered away to a different spot in the lobby. Voss eyed them wonderingly, but with mounting misgivings, for he sensed that something was about to happen. Nervousness gripped him and his mouth was suddenly dry. He swallowed hard, swallowed a second time. He moistened his lips with a quick, nervous darting movement of his tongue. He felt a cold sweat break out over his body.

"Voss," he heard Harp say, and he looked quickly at the judge. "Voss, will you be good enough to ask Milo Sturdevant to come downstairs?"

"Yeah, sure, Judge," he answered, and his voice sounded strangely unfamiliar in his ears.

"Now, please."

Voss started up the stairs.

"If he's asleep," Harp called after him, "wake him."

A minute later when Voss returned and followed Sturdevant down the stairs, Harp was standing at the counter on which a dozen identically sized strips of paper which looked to Voss like bank checks had been laid out together with a freshly pointed pencil. As Sturdevant came off the stairs, a big, burly man whom Voss knew as Chuck stepped behind Sturdevant and deftly lifted the cattleman's gun out of his holster. Sturdevant spun around protestingly, but Chuck grinned at him evilly and, stepping back again, shoved the gun down inside the waistband of his pants. Sturdevant glowered at him, turned and leveled an angry look at Harp.

"Doing things in a pretty high-handed way, aren't you?" he asked.

Harp smiled thinly.

"When my hand is forced," he answered, "I take whatever steps I consider necessary to meet the situation."

"H'm," Sturdevant said, and his lip curled a little.

"I'm frankly disappointed in you, Milo," the judge went on.

"Y'don't say!"

Harp pretended not to notice the sarcasm in Sturdevant's retort.

"I had expected you to show the others the error in their thinking. But you not only failed me there, Milo, now I have good reason to believe you are the prime mover in opposing me and taking a stand against what I asked of you people. But this is unimportant now. Milo, I want ten thousand dollars of you. Mind you, I'm not asking for it. I'm telling you I want it."

"You won't get a goddamned cent outta me!" the cattleman flung back at him. " 'Specially now!"

"And I'm quite certain I will," Harp said quietly. "In fact, I'm so certain, I've gone ahead and prepared a bank draft for that amount." He picked up one of the pieces of paper from the counter. "It's drawn against your account in the Primrose bank. You can sign it in pencil. They told me there it would be acceptable."

"I don't give a damn what they told you!" Sturdevant raged. "I won't sign it!"

"I wish you'd reconsider, Milo."

"I don't have to reconsider anything! I told you I won't sign it, and nothing in the world c'n make me!"

Harp shrugged.

"Perhaps, perhaps not," he said. "However, I think we ought to try. Don't you agree, Chuck?"

The burly man grinned again, even more evilly than before.

"Yeah, sure, Judge," he said.

"Well, then suppose I leave it to you, Chuck, to see what you can do to persuade Mr. Sturdevant to change his mind?"

"Oh, I'll persuade him, all right!"

He came up behind Sturdevant a second time, moving far more swiftly than one would have expected of a man of his size and bulk, clamped a vise-like grip on the cattleman's left wrist and twisted it around behind him and began to force it upward along the rancher's back. Sturdevant struggled to free himself, but his frantic efforts were wasted. Then Chuck hooked his thick right arm around Sturdevant's throat and began to squeeze. Standing back against the wall, Sam Voss paled and began to edge away. When the struggling Sturdevant's face began to redden and a choking, gurgling sound came from him, Harp said: "I think that will do for now, Chuck."

The latter released his hapless victim reluctantly, pushed him up against the counter before he stepped back. Sturdevant, head bowed, his chest and shoulders heaving as he fought to get his breath, clung to the counter.

"The pencil is right in front of you, Milo," Harp said. "And here's the draft for your signature."

He slapped the piece of paper on the counter, picked up the pencil and put it in Sturdevant's right hand.

"Sign it, Milo," he commanded. "If you don't, Chuck will have to repeat his persuasive methods. Only the next time, I won't stop him."

When Sturdevant made no answer and failed to indicate that he intended to comply, Harp beckoned and Chuck came forward again. He grabbed the cattleman's left wrist, tightened his grip on it, and shot a look at Harp.

"Well, Milo?" the judge asked.

Sturdevant, still red-faced and still wheezing, scribbled his name on the draft. Harp smiled, reached and took it from him. Chuck spun Sturdevant around and with a mighty heave sent him careening across the lobby. He collided heavily with the wall, bumped his head on it and slipped down to his knees.

"Get the others down here," Harp ordered, turning to one of his other men.

The man hitched up his levis and trudged upstairs. When the judge motioned, a second man trooped upstairs too and halted at the top of the stairway while the first man marched down the landing. Harp folded the draft that Sturdevant had signed, creased the fold carefully, and put the paper in his pocket. There were loud voices, protesting voices, upstairs; there was the thud of a blow, a cry, then there were massed bootsteps. The first of the herded cattlemen appeared at the head of the stairs. A smear of bright, fresh blood on his mouth indicated that he was the man who had remonstrated and who had been punched. As he came up to Harp's man who was standing there, the latter spun him, pushing him stairward, jerked the gun out of his holster and stepped back again. There was a steady procession after that till eleven cattlemen, all of them disarmed, with wide, wondering eyes, were lined up one behind the other from the stairway to the counter. Each had had a look at Sturdevant huddling head-bent on his knees against the wall. It had the desired effect upon them. Aware of it, Harp pointed to the drafts to be signed and said curtly: "You wouldn't give me what I asked of you, so I'm taking it. These are bank drafts, drawn against your accounts in the Primrose bank. I know to the penny what each of you have on deposit there. I took the trouble to find out. I am mentioning that so there won't be any arguments because I have neither time nor patience for them. Find the draft bearing your name, sign it and hand it to me. Unless you want what our misguided friend Sturdevant got."

Only one man started to protest. He was promptly and painfully jabbed in the stomach by the man in front of him and poked in the back by the man behind him. He flushed a little and averted his eyes when Harp leveled a look at him. When his turn came, he signed the draft awaiting his signature, handed it to the judge without a word, and made no protest when Chuck pushed him stairward again. The line moved steadily, the drafts were signed, and the cattlemen were herded back upstairs. When the last man had gone, Harp nodded to Chuck and walked to the door. Chuck followed him out. The other men sauntered out too a moment later. As the door closed behind him, Voss went quickly to Sturdevant's side.

"You all right, Milo?" he asked, bending over the cattleman.

Sturdevant raised his head, twisted around and slumped back against the wall.

"Yeah, I'm all right," he said. "A mite dizzy. But that's all." Voss helped him to his feet. "Sam," Sturdevant said, "if it's the last thing I do, I'm gonna get that Chuck Cuyler. Nobody's gonna manhandle me and get away with it. And if I ever have the luck to get my hands on that bastard Harp, I'll fix him good!"

They started for the stairs, Voss following Sturdevant mechanically. The latter stopped with his foot on the first step, turned and asked: "You got a gun here?"

"Got a couple of them," Voss replied.

"Good," Sturdevant said, and ordered: "Get them and bring them upstairs."

They parted, the cattleman climbing the stairs and Voss hurrying away through the off-the-lobby door. Minutes later when he reappeared and headed stairward again, he was carrying a rifle and a Colt. Topping the stairs, he hurried down the landing. He did not return. But Sturdevant did. Armed with the Colt, he stood back from the stairway against the wall with a half-raised gun commanding the lobby and the street door. Once when he felt eyes on him, he turned his head and, spotting Voss peering out at him from one of the rooms, he hissed:

" 'Smatter?"

"Nothing," Voss answered. "Just wanted to see if you were all right."

" 'Course I'm all right," Sturdevant retorted indignantly. "You give the rifle to John Gasson?"

"Yeah, sure. He's covering the back yard from the window."

"Tell him not to shoot till he hears me cut loose. Then I want him to open up on those two mavericks watching the back door."

Voss withdrew his head.

But some ten minutes after he poked it out again and hissed at Sturdevant: "P-sst . . . Milo!"

"Yeah?" the cattleman acknowledged grumpily. "What's the matter now?"

"When d'you think Canavan'll be showing up here with your crew?"

Sturdevant frowned.

"You gonna keep pokin' your head out at me every little while to ask me some damned-fool question?" he demanded. Then he hollered: "How the hell should I know when he oughta be showin' up? Just keep your shirt on same's I'm doing, and when you hear all hell break loose outside, you'll know he's back. Now g'wan. Get back inside and stay put there!"

Voss' kitchen clock had just struck twice, and the muffled booming, carrying upstairs, made Sturdevant react to it instinctively. He had been leaning a little wearily against the wall; now he straightened up. Outside there was a blanketing darkness, and a deep, slumbering silence hung over the town. Suddenly there was a startling, hissing sound, and a burning faggot soared upward into the night sky, cutting a fiery path through it, then having reached the top of its climb, it came swishing downward and fell sputtering and still burning in the middle of the gutter in front of the hotel. Three shadowy figures idling on the walk came erect instantly.

"What the hell . . . ?"

"Now where d'you suppose that came from?"

The third man was taken so completely by surprise, it had a paralyzing effect upon him. He stood frozen in his tracks, his eyes wide and staring at the crackling faggot. It flamed brightly, bringing within the range of the light it cast the three men and the building itself. A thunderous blast of gunfire raked the walk and riddled the front of the hotel. When it slackened off for a moment, one man lay sprawled out on the walk, and a second man lay on his side against the building. Curiously though, the third man hadn't been hit at all. Wheeling around toward the door, he yanked out his gun and flung shot after shot at his hidden attackers in an effort to cover his retreat. He reached the door safely, opened it and darted inside only to be met by a burst of gunfire – two, three quick shots that flung him backward. He fell against the opened door, forced himself up again, and turning himself around staggered out. A rifle cracked with an ominous, spiteful hum, and he was hit again. His buckling legs carried him out to the curb. He swayed over it, suddenly pitched out from it and fell in the gutter on his face and belly. There was a wild yell and shadowy figures swarmed out of the alleys opposite the hotel, surged across the street, and splitting into two groups, rounded the building and hurried down the alleys that flanked it.

Now there was another roar of gunfire. This time though it came from farther down the street, from the alleys across the way from the saloon. Its windows shattered and fell in the first volley. There was an answering fire from the saloon's dark depths. A second firebrand that bombed the darkness with its sparks was hurled into the saloon by a man who darted out with it from cover with complete disregard for his safety, and who was probably the least surprised when he managed to scurry back to cover unharmed despite the fact that more than a dozen shots were fired at him. The burning faggot served its purpose. The light from it lit up the place and targeted its defenders for their attackers. Volley after volley was poured into the saloon. The long bar was completely wrecked, and the equally long mirrors that graced the wall behind it were shot to bits. Gaping holes were drilled in both side walls. Ricocheting bullets lost themselves in either the ceiling or the floor. The four ceiling lamps that normally provided the light for the place were shot off the short lengths of polished chain from which they hung. There was a constant musical tinkling as bits, pieces and slivers of glass or glassware spewed out over the floor.

A band of ranchhands, attacking the saloon from the rear, finally broke into the place and drove its defenders streetward. Desperate men seeking to shoot their way out of the closing jaws of the trap were halted once they reached the street and then driven back by blasts of withering gunfire. They were forced to make a stand, and the glass-glittered walk soon ran red with their blood. Man after man was shot down. No quarter was asked and none was given. It was that kind of fight, a fight to a finish. Finally there were but four men left to shoot it out with their attackers, then three, two, and then one. Hit repeatedly, he stood on wide-spread legs and continued to fight back till he emptied his gun. Bending with an unconcealed painful effort, he picked up a fallen man's gun. But before he could straighten up and level it, another blast of gunfire bracketed and riddled him. He was dead before he struck the ground. There was an authoritative yell of "Hold it!" The shooting stopped abruptly, and a strange stillness draped itself over the scene. It lasted for perhaps half a minute. When there was another yell, this time of "All right, men! That's it!" there was massed movement. The alleys began to empty themselves as armed men, with the throbbing excitement of the fighting still making their blood race, spilled out into the street. Some of them trudged into the battered saloon, apparently curious to see what havoc they had wrought upon it. The faggot, burning itself out, lay on the floor a step or two inside the doorway. The first man to enter ground it out. Someone had stumbled upon some lanterns standing in an out-of-the-way corner, and they were snatched up, quickly lighted and handed out.

A man who had halted in the very middle of the saloon surveyed the wreckage and said with a mournful shake of his head: "Now there isn't any place left where a feller can buy himself a drink when he wants one."

"Won't be that way for long, partner," another man assured him. "The saloon business is just about the best-payin' business in the world. So you can bet on it somebody'll take over the place once things quiet down around here and before you know it, it'll be right back the way it was before we shot the hell out of it. Meanwhile think of all the dough you'll be saving not being able to spend it over the bar."

"Huh," the first man said with a scornful twist of his lips; he wheeled around and stalked out.

Another man with a lantern swinging from his hand tramped out, and raising the lantern, spread light over the bloodied, glass-strewn walk. Grotesquely sprawled-out and hunched-over bodies lay here and there. With light to see by, men gathered around the spot, and while some stood back, others moved among the dead – apparently eager to see the faces of those who had fallen before their guns – and began to ease them over on their backs. A man appeared in the doorway and hollered: "Hey, anybody see Canavan around?"

Eyes lifted and focused on him questioningly.

"Who'd you say, Mac? Canavan?"

"Yeah. Big, red-headed feller."

"He was around here a while ago," somebody said.

"Think I saw him going up the street," somebody else added. "Up toward the hotel."

There were drumming hoofbeats upstreet and heads turned in their direction.

"Maybe that's him coming now," someone suggested.

"So blamed dark," someone else

complained, "I can only make out the horse, but not the feller ridin' him."

The horseman came closer.

"That you, Canavan?" a man yelled.

"Yeah!"

"Somebody here wants to see you!"

Canavan slowed Aggie to a trot as he neared the saloon, then to a mere walk as he came up to it. He halted the mare at the curb and swung down, crossed the littered walk and entered the saloon. The man who had called for him stopped him and asked: "You know Mike Hoban?"

Canavan nodded, and asked: "What about him?"

"Found him layin' in the back so shot up, looked to me like somebody must've emptied a gun into him. Hit him a couple o' times in the belly, and at least once in the chest and in the shoulder. I thought he was dead, the way he was layin' there. But when I touched him, he came to. Asked if you were around and said he wanted to see you before he cashed in. And from the looks of him, I don't think that's far off. Come on. I'll show you where he is."

Canavan followed the man to the rear. In a small side room with a portiere-covered doorway, four men, one of them holding a lighted lantern above the sprawled-out figure of a man who lay against the wall, were standing about, apparently waiting for Canavan or for the man who had gone to call him. Blood that had seeped out of the fallen man's body ran along the cracks between the floorboards and shone where the lantern light struck it. The man who was holding the lantern lifted his eyes, met Canavan's and shook his head. Canavan came up beside him and bent over Hoban. The latter's eyes were closed. There was a thin smear of blood on his lips and blood bubbled in his nostrils. His shirtfront was blood soaked.

"Mike," Canavan said.

Hoban's lids fluttered, then his eyes opened. He managed a thin, fleeting, mouth-twitching grin of recognition.

"Oh, h'llo, Mac," he whispered.

Canavan bent a little lower.

"I've been wondering about you, Mike."

"I've been around. Only Harp kinda soured on me and kept me outta things like he was afraid you an' me were too friendly for his good and maybe that I might turn on him and join up with you against him." Hoban stopped, apparently having run out of breath. His chest heaved, and he sucked in air through his open mouth. After a moment, he added: "He's gone, Mac."

"I know," Canavan told him. "Leastways, that's what I figured."

Hoban gave no sign that he had heard Canavan. His eyes closed gently. But after a moment they opened again, about halfway.

"Yeah, he rode outta here headed for Primrose about an hour ago." Hoban's voice was very faint now and Canavan had to bend lower to catch what he was saying. "He took Chuck Cuyler with him. If you get going, you oughta be able to catch up with them easy. Harp isn't much on a horse. Scared of horses and shows it. Rides like he thinks the horse is gonna buck him off any minute. So he won't be travelin' too fast. And that Chuck, Mac. I never did cotton to that one. Never liked him or his looks. You oughta be able to shoot holes in him before he even gets his gun out, he's that slow coming up with it. Yeah, slower'n molasses."

Again Hoban stopped, and again his eyes closed. He did not open them again.

"I knew when he lit outta here," he went on shortly, his voice just a murmur, "he wouldn't be coming back. Knew he didn't intend to. Even though he kept telling everybody he would. And you shoulda heard him tellin' everybody that nothing was gonna happen, that the cattlemen were too scared of him to do anything, that when he got back he was gonna let us in on the big plans he'd made for him and for us too. The weasely little bastard. He knew the cattlemen wouldn't let him ride roughshod over them for long. And he musta known in his heart he was running out on us. But there wasn't anything we could do about it 'cept stay put here and fight and . . . and die. And that's the way it's worked out. Mac . . ."

"Yeah, Mike?"

When Hoban did not go on, the man with the lantern held it a little lower over him. He looked hard at him, then he eased back and lifted his gaze to Canavan and shook his head.

"Going fast now," he said out of a corner of his mouth. "Another couple o' minutes and that'll be it."

The dying man's lips moved. But no sound came from him. His big, burly body relaxed and seemed to sink lower and spread itself. Another man, one who had been standing by silently and just looking on, bent over him, peered hard at him, came erect again and stepping back, said: "That's it for him, all right. The end of the trail."

Slowly Canavan straightened up. There was a faint, gentle murmuring sound from Hoban as his breath ebbed out of his riddled body. Then he lay very still.

"He's dead," the man holding the lantern said simply.

"Yeah," another man said. "He had it coming to him, I suppose. Even though he wasn't as bad as the others in Harp's crew. I wonder what he did that made him hightail it from the law?"

"What difference does that make, what he did?" still another man retorted. "Far as we're concerned, he was guilty of one thing. Of joining up with Harp. So what the rest of Harp's gang got, he had to get too. That's the only way to look at it. Right, Canavan?"

Canavan didn't answer. He stood motionlessly for a moment, then he turned on his heel and went out. He strode through the saloon and out to the street, to the impatiently waiting and ground-pawing mare, disregarded the frankly curious stares that were leveled at him, and climbed up on Aggie's back. He wheeled her away from the low curb, threaded his way through and around the little bunches of men who were idling about now in the gutter, and when he was clear of them, he nudged Aggie with his knees and she responded, loped downstreet at a steadily quickening pace. By the time she reached the corner, she was running in full stride. She took the upgrade at a gallop and, topping it, dashed away westward.

Dawn had just broken over the range when Canavan awoke. A gray and drab dawn it was too; the air was damp and bone-chilling, the grass about him dew-beaded. He sat up, hunched over and huddled in his blanket. Unhappily he knew there would be no breakfast for him that morning. He could not afford to chance being betrayed by a campfire even though he was sorely tempted and would have given much for a cup of steaming hot coffee. Reluctantly then he kicked off the blanket and got up on his feet. He stamped about for a minute or two in an effort to get the blood circulating through his stiffened body. He stopped and stretched mightily, yawned and stretched again. He turned as Aggie came trotting up to him. He put his arms around her neck, and she whinnied delightedly and nuzzled him. Then pushing her off, he picked up his saddle and hoisted it onto her back, bent and buckled the cinches under her belly, rolled up the blanket and strapped it on behind the saddle, and climbed up astride the mare. She trotted away with him. The veiling shadows, he noticed, were beginning to lift and dissolve, revealing the raw grimness of the hushed rangeland, and bringing more and more far-flung stretches of open country into view.

From time to time he rose up in the stirrups

and took a quick, searching look about him. But there were no signs yet of his quarries. However, they couldn't be too far ahead of him, he told himself. An hour's head start might have meant something, a serious and possibly an insurmountable handicap had everything between them and himself been equal. But they weren't; hence he wasn't overly concerned. He was confident that Aggie could outrun any horse on the range, and certainly he was a far better rider than either Harp or the massive Chuck Cuyler. Remembering what the dying Mike Hoban had told him about the judge's horsemanship, he was sure that Harp must have found night riding much too hazardous for him and that he must have insisted upon calling a halt for the night, particularly if his horse resisted Harp's attempts to hold him down to a slow pace. Then too, because Harp had no reason to suspect that he was being pursued, he would not push on too vigorously. He would take his time, riding by day and laying over at night. He would find them soon enough, Canavan assured himself. Perhaps even before he actually came upon them their campfire would betray their campsite. He glanced skyward for signs of lazy, curling smoke, but there were none.

A mile slipped away behind him, then a

second and a third. And suddenly Aggie stopped, and he looked up instantly. What he saw made him shake his head. A couple of hundred feet away two tethered horses were grazing peacefully off the road, and fairly close by them lay two blanketed figures.

"I coulda had a whole potful of good, hot coffee," he muttered half aloud, "only I didn't want to take a chance lighting a fire that they might see. And lookit the way I find them. Sleepin' away like good fellers. Like they didn't have a care in the world, or a thing on their consciences."

He guided Aggie off the road and into the thick, muffling grass that flanked it, and held her to a walk as he approached the sleeping men. Fifty feet from them he pulled up and dismounted and said to the mare: "Stay put here, Aggie. Y'hear?"

Apparently she heard, and understood too, for she tossed her head in a sort of nodding motion. He patted her and walked on. His right hand dropped and curled around the butt of his gun, ready for an instant draw if he discovered that his quarries were aware of his presence and were merely pretending to be asleep. The grazing horses lifted their heads and eyed him as he came toward them, but they made no sound and went back to their grass-munching. Slowing his step as he neared the blanketed figures, and watching them alertly, he circled around to a point beyond their heads. Backing off a couple of steps, he eased himself down on his haunches with his gun still holding on Harp and Cuyler. He fired suddenly over their heads. There was instant reaction to it, frightened reaction. Both men threw off their blankets and sat up and looked about them with wide, startled eyes.

"You've both looked everywhere 'cept back here," Canavan said. Harp's head jerked around instantly, then Cuyler's did. The blood drained out of the former's face when he saw Canavan. Cuyler scowled darkly. "Hated to have to wake you two sleepin' beauties, but it's business before pleasure, you know. You, Cuyler. Keep your fat, grubby paw away from your gun. Y'hear? Somebody back in Paradise, a thin, scrawny old-timer named Sturdevant who didn't like the way you manhandled him, asked me to do him a favor when I caught up with you and put a slug in you for him. You get any ideas, and I'll do just that, and with pleasure too. Now both of you get up on your feet and come up with your hands high. Where I can see them. Come on. Up on your hind legs."

"Just a minute, Canavan," Harp said. "What do you want of us?"

"For one thing," Canavan answered, "a batch of bank drafts."

"And in return for them?"

"Nothing. I'm not here to make a deal with you. You'll hand over those drafts, or I'll take them from you. You decide which it's to be. Although I kinda think I'd prefer to have to take them. Dig them out, Harp."

"Hold it a minute, partner," Cuyler said.

"Don't you call me partner, you overstuffed butcher."

Chuck Cuyler's face flamed.

"Get out those drafts, Harp," Canavan commanded, "and toss them over to me."

Harp was motionless for a moment, then twisting around he thrust one hand deep inside his blanket, and reached for something. Twisting around again, clumsily because of the suddenness with which he did it, he came up with a gun. But before he could level it and shoot, Canavan's gun thundered protestingly. Harp cried out and dropped the gun and made a grab with his left hand for his blood-spurting right wrist. It was Cuyler's turn then, and as he came up with his hastily, clumsily drawn gun, Canavan's Colt roared a second time. Chuck didn't cry out when he was hit as Harp had done; he cursed instead, and dropped his gun as though it had suddenly gotten too hot to hold, stared for a moment at his right wrist, stared in fascination at the blood that was spouting from it and running freely over his hand. A thin wisp of blue smoke curled upward gently from the blackened nozzle of the Colt, and, mushrooming when it lofted and caromed off the brim of Canavan's hat, began to dissolve.

"Well," he said, shuttling his gaze between Harp and Cuyler. "Looks to me like that's it."

He stood erect then and sauntered over to the two crouching men. He hauled Harp to his feet, thrust his hand inside the judge's coat, and when he withdrew his hand, he was clutching a batch of evenly folded and neatly creased bank drafts. He put them in his own pocket. He picked up Harp's gun and flung it away. Then he crossed behind the judge to Cuyler's side, collared him and dragged him to his feet, and stepped back from him.

"All right, you two," he said curtly and authoritatively, gesturing with his gun. "Let's go."

"Where ... where are you taking us?" Harp faltered.

The sight of blood, even his own, apparently sickened him for his face had taken on a sickish hue.

"Where?" Canavan repeated. "Where d'you think? Back to Paradise, of course.

The folks there have some unfinished business they'd like to finish with you. 'Specially some storekeepers who claim you took some money that belongs to them and they want it back. As for your friend here, somebody told me he's wanted back in Texas for a couple o' murders. Being that Sturdevant owes him something, he thinks a good way for him to square accounts would be by seeing to it personally that Cuyler gets back to Texas safely. That's it. Let's go."

It was the following morning. Outside the stable Canavan was saddling Aggie as a glum-looking Christopher Daws looked on. Canavan shot a look at the stocky newspaperman, straightened up and said: "Anybody looking at you would think the world was coming to an end. We set out to do something and we made it come off, didn't we? So don't look like that."

"I wish you'd reconsider Sturdevant's offer," Daws urged earnestly. "He's willing to throw in an extra fifty dollars a month if you'll stay on and take the sheriff's job. That makes it about as good-paying a job as any you'll ever find."

"I know, Daws. But I don't want it."

"What's so pressing in California?" Daws wanted to know.

"I'm looking for something," Canavan replied, "and I think that's where I'll find it."

"H'm," Daws said.

"Remember the first time we met, when you stopped me goin' by your place, and you thought I was a lawman?"

"Of course I remember it."

"I didn't tell you this, but I was a lawman once. A Texas Ranger as a matter of fact. But I was kicked out."

Daws stared at him.

"Kicked out?" he echoed. "I . . . I don't believe it!"

"It's true though. I was kicked out because I took the law into my own hands and killed five men."

Daws' wide eyes held on him. Now his mouth opened and his jaw hung.

"Y'see, my wife was expectin' a baby. Would've been our first and we were both looking forward to it like a couple of kids who know something nice is on the way to them and are beginning to run out of patience waiting for it to show up. I was away on an assignment when I got a letter from Beth saying she'd decided to go visit some relatives of hers. I'd just wound up the job I'd been sent to do and I'd already telegraphed Ranger headquarters asking for orders. Instead, being that I had some time off coming to me, they told me to go home for a couple of weeks. But I got the bright idea of heading for Beth's kinfolks' place, to surprise her, and when she was set to head back home, I figured I'd ride back with her instead of letting her do it by herself."

Canavan paused and moistened his lips with his tongue.

"But when I got there, to her relatives' place, I found the place had been burned to the ground. Beth and her cousins were dead. Shot down in cold blood when they tried to break out of the burning house. I guess I just about went crazy when I heard the story. There were five men responsible for it and I got every one of them."

"Despite the fact that you were fully justified in doing what you did, they still kicked you out?"

Canavan nodded.

"The law's the law, and it has to be upheld, justification or no. Anyway, I've done nothing these past six years. Just knocked around. Couldn't do anything because I was too restless, had to keep moving about. That's bad for a man. Everybody needs to do something, needs to take root somewhere and grow. I think I've got the restlessness out of my system by now, and I'm about ready to take root somewhere."

"Well?" Daws asked eagerly. "Then can I go and tell Sturdevant that you've changed your mind and that . . . ?"

Canavan shook his head.

"No, Daws," he said. "It's still California for me. It's new, big, rich country out there, and all the opportunity any man could ask for. So that's where I'm going."

"Damn," Daws said unhappily.

Canavan patted him on the back.

"When I get set out there, I'll let you know where to send me that newspaper of yours. It'll be nice reading about Paradise and some of the people I've met here." He held out his hand to Daws. "So long, partner. Keep the presses rolling."

They gripped hands, then Canavan turned and climbed up on Aggie's back.

" 'Bye," he called as he rode down the street.

"Canavan!" he heard someone cry and he pulled up instantly and looked around.

Ardis Lundy was standing at the curb in front of Daws' place. Canavan wheeled the mare and rode back, wheeled again in front of her, and slacked a little in the saddle.

"Off again?" she asked, her voice tinged with sarcasm.

"That's right," Canavan answered gravely.

"And when will you be back?"

"I won't be back."

"What do you mean, you won't be back?"

"Just that, Ardis. I'm heading for California."

"But what . . . what about me?"

"What about you?"

"Well, have you made any arrangements for me?"

"Nope," he said evenly.

"Well, don't you think you ought to?"

"Nope," he said again.

"Then what am I supposed to do?"

"That's up to you. The stores will be opening again in a couple of days, and I think you oughta start looking around for a job. Whatever will pay you enough to live on. But as I said before, that's up to you."

"But . . . but suppose I can't get a job?"

"That'll be your problem, lady. Not mine."

He straightened up in the saddle, tightened his grip on the reins, nudged Aggie with his knees, and as he trotted away, he twisted around and called: " 'Bye, Ardis, and good luck!"

"No!" she screamed and lifting her skirts, stepped down into the gutter and ran after him. "Wait! You can't leave me like this! You can't shirk your responsibility!"

He didn't answer. He settled himself, and

Aggie quickened her pace. Canavan looked back once more. Ardis had faltered to a stumbling stop. Lifting her skirts again, she started to run again. She tripped and fell: when he pulled up and wheeled around, she got up and ran even faster than before. Satisfied then that she hadn't really hurt herself, Canavan was about to ride on. But Aggie had been watching the oncoming Ardis, and, deciding that things had gone far enough, she took matters into her own hands. She swung around and galloped downstreet, disregarded Ardis' scream that she could hear somewhere behind her, and pounded up the incline. Topping the upgrade, she paused for an instant, raised her head and trumpeted scornfully. Then she dashed away.

The publishers hope that this book has given you enjoyable reading. Large Print Books are specially designed to be as easy to see and hold as possible. If you wish a complete list of our books, please ask at your local library or write directly to: Curley Publishing, Inc., P.O. Box 37, South Yarmouth, Massachusetts, 02664.